THE FROST AND
THE FIRE

by

GLORIA BEVAN

HARLEQUIN BOOKS   TORONTO
WINNIPEG

Original hard cover edition published in 1973
by Mills & Boon Limited, 17-19 Foley Street,
London W1A 1DR, England

© Gloria Bevan 1973

SBN 373-01682-4

Harlequin edition published May, 1973

Printed in Canada

THE girl seated at the wheel of the big old car raised an anxious glance towards the rear-vision mirror as the creaking horse-float behind her lurched around yet another fern-encrusted bend on the road cut through glistening New Zealand bush.

The brief glimpse of the chestnut's flowing mane assured her that her mount was as steadily balanced as ever. Liz had endured a few uneasy moments on the journey on his account. The float was awfully old, almost falling apart really, and if anything should go wrong on this lonely bush track with its steep grades and winding bends ... but of course Red was accustomed to travelling in the float and despite his colouring wasn't a temperamental type. After all, he was no longer a skittish two-year-old.

Liz concentrated her attention on the red clay and rough metal of the road ahead, swerving sharply in order to avoid a wash-out left from winter rains, where the road edge crumbled away to the edge of tea-tree-covered slopes dropping hundreds of feet to a gully below.

A fragment of metal thrown up from the roadway struck the undercarriage of the vehicle with a dull thud. Tattered toa-toas leaning at drunken angles along the highway tossed their feathery plumes in the breeze as the old car whined around a hairpin bend. She was fast becoming accustomed to the sheer drops on either side, the red clay banks where tall pungas raised their tightly curled fronds against the blue. She would just *have* to get used to the road now that she had committed herself to a stay in this unknown area where the dusty winding bush track would be her main link with the outside world.

A bank of billowing gunmetal-coloured clouds drifted over the sun, ahead of her stretched an undeviating length of highway. Liz relaxed against the tattered upholstery of the sagging seat and reviewed the situation. It seemed an ideal time for her to make a change from city living, now that her friend and flat-mate Mary had left the district to be married to a farmer in another part of the country. And after her own break with Leon ... unconsciously she sighed. Well, she wasn't the first girl to be let down by someone she'd trusted, to find she had been stupid enough to fall in love with a man who preferred someone else. If only he had told her when it all happened, instead of letting her go blithely on hoping, planning, dreaming. Oh, she should have guessed right from the beginning that a sophisticate such as Leon would choose as his wife a girl more his own type. Someone like Elaine, a fashion model with flair and finesse. Not a girl who was nuts about the country and whose tastes ran to shows and hunts and gymkhanas, things like that. Or was that merely an excuse she had dreamed up to ease the sense of bewilderment and let-down? Once again she found herself back on the dreary treadmill of her thoughts. It's over, she reminded herself sternly. It was over six months ago. *You're* over it too. Why, there were times now when Leon didn't enter her thoughts for days at a time. Her soft curving lips tightening. One thing was for sure—if that was all love was about, misery and disillusionment and heartache, she was done with it! As from today she would concentrate on other things, seek new interests. For a start, this new venture that she was entering into—thanks to Uncle Harry! She sent up a tiny silent prayer of thanks to the relative whose legacy had made it possible for her to make a dream come true. Well, not quite, not yet, but she intended to give it a darned good help along the way!

Funny to think that the first tiny advertisement under the heading Property for Sale she had found in the local newspaper had proved to be the single one that she could afford even to consider purchasing.

Forty acres, it said, with cottage, outbuildings, ponies, *suitable riding school.* Liz had felt excited merely by reading about it. At the incredibly low price at which the property was valued she would have sufficient funds left over from Uncle Harry's money (somehow she always thought of it that way) to cover the necessary expenses in getting her venture off the ground and allow for her modest living costs. By being very economical, she wouldn't require a lot of new frocks and slacks out there in the bush and she had plenty of riding gear, she should be able to run the place as she wanted to for a year. If at the end of the period it proved to be successful, chances were that someone else would be willing to carry on with the work, once the riding school had been proved a workable proposition. If only the property weren't too far distant from town for her purposes. Rangiwahia ... the soft Maori syllables sounded so remote. When, however, she put through a telephone call to the solicitor who was handling the property sale, the place transpired to be not so far away from town after all, a small farming area on Auckland's wild and rugged west coast. The previous tenant, the dry legal tones informed her, had intended using the property as a riding school, so if that was what Miss Kennedy had in mind——?

'Oh, it is! It is!' she assured him in her husky eager tones.

In that case she would need to make up her mind immediately as another client was anxious to purchase the land, but she had made the first enquiry so, if she were interested ...

Miss Kennedy was more than interested, she made up her mind at that moment to acquire the place that promised to be ideal for her purposes and that happened, wonder of wonders, to be available at a price she could afford.

On the following day the legal agreement was duly drawn up, signed and witnessed and Liz found herself in possession of forty acres of land, cottage, various outbuildings, two ponies. Before taking up residence on the property, however, there were matters in town that must be attended to. She would need to hand in her notice to the director of the Crippled Children's Institute where she worked with small cerebral palsy patients. There was her hunter Red to be shod and the flat to be vacated. Her few pieces of furniture would have to be transported to the cottage at Rangiwahia.

When later in the day Liz put through a phone call to her older sister Helen, living in a town a hundred miles south, she found the telephone connection disappointingly bad. 'Look,' she caught Helen's clear, precise tones, 'I can't hear a word you're saying, but I gather you're thinking of making a change. Don't do anything until we've had a chat about it. I've got to come to Auckland some time soon, Alan wants me to do some business in town for him, so I'll catch the afternoon plane.'

She was as good as her word, arriving at the flat as Liz finished laying the small table for two. On being informed of the projected venture, Helen was anything but enthusiastic.

'I think you're mad,' she announced with sisterly candour. 'Rushing off to the back of beyond without even stopping to think! It's Uncle Harry's legacy that's given you these wild ideas! I bet he'd never have left you a cent if he'd guessed what you planned to do with the money!'

'He would, you know! He often told me that if anyone wanted to invest their capital in this country they couldn't ever go wrong by putting it into property.'

'Not if the property happens to be in the outback with a name that no one's ever even heard of. What did you say it was called?'

'Rangiwahia. And what do you think it means in the Maori language? You'd never believe it! "An invalid getting better" or "sunshine breaking through a rift in the clouds!" Anyway, it's just the place for me.' She laughed. 'What I mean is, that's the whole idea of the riding centre. To give the handicapped kids a chance, let them have just for once, a place in the sun!'

Helen smiled her superior elder-sister smile. 'Long

8

on sunshine, short on everything else—that's what it'll be like. You'll see. There'll be no shops, no amenities, nothing . . . remote as can be.'

'Not really,' Liz pointed out reasonably. 'It's not all that many miles out of town.'

'On those winding west coast roads,' Helen retorted grimly, 'a few miles can mean quite a step!' Her calm blue eyes were fixed on Liz's animated face. 'What gets me is why you're taking on all this?'

'Why?' The great dark eyes were thoughtful. 'I guess it's just something I've always wanted to do, ever since I started work with the disabled kids. It's been at the back of my mind for ages, but I never mentioned it to anyone before. There didn't seem much point when I couldn't do anything about it. Then when old Uncle Harry, bless his kind heart, left us equal shares of his money, wow! That did it!'

'Disabled kids?' Helen's thin face with its chiselled features wore a puzzled expression. 'But I thought you were planning to set up a riding school out there on the coast. What on earth are you talking about?'

Liz sighed impatiently. 'I keep telling and *telling* you! It's this idea of mine! I know, I just *know*, that if some of the spastic children could be got up on a horse, have a chance of being taught to ride, it would work miracles for them. They'd feel they could do something that ordinary kids could do. It would build up their confidence in a way nothing else could. Once they got to riding without any fear, were really relaxed, then they'd be willing to have a go at other things . . . maybe get themselves up on crutches, try out something else that they never dreamed they could manage to do. It would be terrific for them in other ways too—exercise out in the open air, mobility, a complete change out in the country. It's something I've been longing to do for so long, but now I've got it all worked out,' the warm husky tones ran on. 'I've got permission from the doctors to have the children brought out to the horses. It'll be quite a thing, really . . . involve ambulances, drivers, therapists as well as the medical men at the beginning to make sure there'll

9

be no danger. I'm planning to have a special timber railing put up where the children can be lifted up on to the back of the ponies——'

'A crippled child wouldn't be able to balance himself on a pony——'

'He would if he had someone to lead the pony and a helper on each side of him to keep him steady by holding on to a special safety belt——'

'What helpers?' It seemed that Helen was bent on being discouraging.

Liz waved a careless hand. 'Friends, relatives, anyone who I can get to come along for a day and lend a hand! If I can't find helpers any other way I'll put an ad in the city newspapers, make an announcement asking for them, over television and radio. Some of the helpers could bring the children out from town in their private cars and that would help too.'

Helen's mind, however, appeared to be working along entirely different lines. 'It's a crazy scheme! You never stop to think what could happen——'

'I know.' Liz flashed her quick smile. 'That's half the fun of things, not knowing. Anyway,' she lifted a small square chin, 'who said it was crazy? The doctors and therapists I spoke to about it think it's a tremendous idea. They said it was something well worth trying out, that it could make all the difference in the world to these handicapped kids. And that would be just the start! If it's a success, and I *know* it will be, it could be extended later to include lots of other disabled children ... blind ... deaf ... they'd all require different types of treatment, of course, but they could all benefit by it. Just imagine it, Helen,' the dark eyes glowed, 'a full-time riding centre for the disabled!'

'You must get it from Dad,' Helen murmured morosely. 'You were too young to remember him much, but he was like you, always dreaming up some grand scheme or other, wanting to sell up everything to finance a hare-brained idea, a mythical oil well, or something. It was lucky he had Mum to keep his feet firmly on the ground. If only,' she wailed, 'you had asked Alan about it first. He would never have let you rush into a thing like this blindfold.'

'I know he wouldn't,' Liz grinned cheerfully. 'That's why I wanted to do it this way. Oh, I know Alan would have known about all the financial angles,' she added quickly, for Helen's face had fallen. Liz was well aware that in her sister's opinion there was no one who could match her husband in the matter of business acumen. 'It was just that I wanted to handle it myself.'

'You don't mean to tell me——?' Helen's small mouth had dropped open. 'You haven't actually paid over the money?'

Liz nodded. 'So it's too late to worry about it. For me it had to be Rangiwahia—or nowhere at all. I knew I'd never get a chance of any other block of land that distance from town at the price, not in a hundred years!'

'If you got forty acres of land for the money Uncle Harry left you there must be something wrong with it——'

'Less——'

'Then there *is* a catch in it! Liz, how *could* you be such an utter idiot?'

'You're wrong, you know. The solicitor rang me at work and told me all about it. The place is all in grass and there's a cottage I can live in. A caretaker and his wife have it at the moment, but there are three bedrooms, so it must be fairly roomy. And what do you know? There was someone else trying to buy it too, on the same day! I had to make up my mind right away. It'll be all right, honestly,' for Helen's smooth brow was furrowed. 'The previous owners intended using the place as a riding school. The barns and outbuildings are already there. There are even a couple of ponies and a certain amount of riding gear, so the solicitor told me.'

'Solicitors don't always tell all.'

'Oh well, if there were anything terribly wrong I could always sell again. You can't lose out on land, especially at this low figure.'

'Don't be too sure. There's a catch in it, you'll see.'

Liz could almost see her sister's mind turning over. 'It seems to me that this project you're so carried away with is some sort of charity work. How can you possibly expect to make a living out of that?'

'Oh, I don't!'

'Now I know you're mad! Just how do you intend to live?'

Liz, however, had an answer to that one too. 'I can manage, for a year. I've thought it all out.' Her eyes were shining, excited. 'I've enough money saved from my wages at the Institute to keep me going for twelve months. If things get tough I might even think about taking a few ordinary children for rides at the weekends. Adults too, so long as they'd be happy with a ride in the country. I won't be geared for instruction. It would be better for the ponies, keep them in trim.' Ignoring Helen's tightly compressed lips, she swept happily on. 'It'll be great for Red too. Just think, no more being tossed out of grazing paddocks every few weeks. He'll have swags of gorgeous green grass, fresh country air for a change, swims in the surf. He just won't know himself——'

'I wasn't thinking about Red,' Helen cut in impatiently, her voice sharp with disapproval. 'When did you say you intended going to this peculiar set-up?'

'Next week.'

'Next week!' Helen's voice was a horrified squeak. 'Isn't that just like you! Impulsive to the point of idiocy! Oh, I don't mean it isn't a good idea for the spastic children,' she added quickly. 'I guess it would give them confidence and get them out in the open air and all that, but why can't someone else do it, some charitable organisation with loads of funds?'

Liz shook her dark head. 'There is no one else. If I don't carry it through the scheme won't ever get started. This is my chance to give it a go.'

'Bet you haven't even been out to see the place?'

'There hasn't been time, and anyway, I don't need to. If it's suitable for a riding place and there are some ponies and somewhere to live, that's good enough for me.'

Helen's blue eyes rose ceilingwards. '"Don't need to," she says! Why, it could be anything! That's you all over, burning your bridges behind you, not giving yourself time to think, tossing away a good job to rush off on some wild scheme just because you're sorry for the children. I'm sorry for spastic children too, so is everyone else, but——' She broke off and added after a moment, 'You just don't care about the things that really matter.'

'Such as?' Liz got up to help herself to an apple from the sideboard and perching herself on the edge of the table, swung a slim tanned leg.

'If only,' sighed Helen, 'you'd think about getting married.'

'Oh, that . . .' Liz turned her head aside before her sister, with her uncanny knack of guessing her secrets, could catch the shadow that had clouded her eyes. Thank heaven Helen had no inkling of how many times all through last year she had dreamed of marriage. It was Leon, she mused bleakly, who hadn't given the subject a thought, at least not so far as she was concerned.

Helen's thoughtful gaze rested on her young sister. Petite and dark with enormous brown eyes that mirrored every change of expression. A clean jawline and that small delightfully curved mouth. Long dark hair caught carelessly back from a centre parting by a rubber band. An impeccably neat person herself, conscientious over the slightest detail of her appearance, Helen sighed exasperatedly as she took in the clear skin, innocent of make-up, the schoolgirlish white cotton blouse open at the throat, faded blue hipster jeans, rubber thongs on bare tanned feet.

'It's not as if men aren't attracted to you,' she admitted reluctantly. 'They are, somehow. Must have something to do with that wide-eyed stare of yours. Makes you look about seventeen, instead of twenty-two.'

For answer Liz opened her brown eyes wider, wrinkling her short straight nose in derision.

'If only you'd meet some nice man . . . it's not as

though you don't have opportunities.'

Liz nibbled a long strand of dark hair in an unconscious gesture. 'But I do——'

'Once or twice maybe, and that's it! The trouble
with you is that you just don't *try*! Take Neville, next
door to me,' Helen swept on as Liz opened her mouth
in protest. 'Ever since that holiday you spent with us
he's been quite wrapped up in you. He's everlastingly
ringing me up, hinting that I write and ask you down
for a weekend. All the time you were in the room he
couldn't seem to take his eyes from you. You *must* have
noticed!'

Liz grinned unrepentantly. 'Oh, I noticed all right!
That's why I haven't been down to stay lately.'

'No, you wouldn't! You never ever do the right
thing for yourself.' You could tell by her tone, Liz
thought, that she knew she was beaten, but still Helen
pressed doggedly on. 'If you'd only be sensible, play
your cards right, you could have a well-paid nursing
job in town, Neville, a nice house in the suburbs. Why
don't you think about it?'

Briefly Liz thought about Neville, his neatly-parted
auburn hair and the suburban life that he was no
doubt planning to offer her in his neat accountant's
mind, then dismissed him from her thoughts.

'I told you before,' Helen said, 'you're just not
interested.'

'And the trouble with you,' retorted Liz, laughing,
'is that you've got this thing about marriage. Just because you've got a nice man like Alan for yourself
you're always trying to con everyone else into getting
married too. But heavens to Betsy—Neville!'

'He'd make any girl a wonderful husband.'
husky laugh and slipped down from the table.

'Any other girl, maybe!' Liz laughed her warm

'I just can't understand you,' her sister burst out.
'You'll never meet anyone out there on that wild
coast,' she prophesied gloomily. 'There's no one out
there to meet. I went for a drive to the Coast once and
believe me, it's just about the end of the world. Nothing but high cliffs, breakers pounding in on miles of

black sand, thick bush——'

'——Lovely quiet roads for the kids to ride on,' Liz reminded her happily.

She was accustomed to Helen's dire warnings of disaster and forgot them immediately they were uttered, in much the same way that as children she had become used to her elder sister's protective attitude. She supposed it stemmed from both girls having lost their parents when they were so young, Helen a child of ten, Liz only a baby. But golly, to hear her talk, anyone would think Helen was her mother! Neville indeed!

No matter what Helen said on the subject, or any-one else for that matter, she intended to take a chance of the opportunity that fate had sent her way. Even if monetary rewards were non-existent, at least it would be work that would be satisfying and worth while. On the coast, and in the country too! She could almost smell the salty tang of the sea, the fragrance of wild flowers and grasses. It would be a fresh start for her, doing work she enjoyed with children to whom life had given a raw deal. In a way it would be a sort of holiday, and even if things didn't turn out quite as well as she hoped, well, she'd have given it a go, and a year wasn't for ever.

The next moment she swung around a bend and forgot everything else in the scene that met her gaze.

A haze of spray veiled towering black sandhills and in the sweep of bay with its wide expanse of dark sand, sunlight pinpointed a myriad sequins in the glittering ironsands, From the beach a narrow jagged pinnacle soared high against a backdrop of high flax-covered hills, and beyond gleamed the misty blue of the Tasman. All at once she was struck by a sense of remoteness. There was nothing but the wind tracing patterns in drifting sand, waves thundering in a shower of spray on a wide expanse of black sand, the endless dull boom of the surf.

As she ran the car down a narrow path and turned into a patch of lush green grass in the shade of giant gnarled pohutukawa trees, Liz decided to break her journey and take a swim in this lonely bay. Now that she had reached the coast she couldn't be far from her destination, and a dip in the cool blueness was just what she needed to dispel the heat and dust of the winding bush roads.

A swift search through her shabby travel bag made her realise that she had forgotten to include in her luggage swimsuit or bikini. No matter, they would arrive later with the furniture in the transporter. Meantime she would go in the water in the drip-dry shirt and shorts she was wearing. The hot sunshine would dry out her garments in time for her to arrive at the property looking fairly presentable. Not, of course, the way in which Helen would reach a new destination, but still . . .

A check of the horse in the float assured her that the chestnut had suffered no ill effects from the journey. 'Won't be long, feller!' With a friendly pat on the sturdy neck she turned away and made her way over drifts of burning black sand, cooling her feet in a fresh water stream flowing down from the high, flax-covered hills above. Then, ploughing her way over the sand-hills where marram grass retained its precarious hold, she moved towards the stretch of sand where chequered red and yellow flags fluttered their message indicating an area of the beach that was safe for swimmers.

At last her feet touched cool wet sand, still flecked with fragments of foam left from the last breaker. Liz ran into a cloud of spray, enjoying the crisp tang of the water as a wave carried her away from the shore. It was invigorating, exhilarating, altogether a delight. She felt she never wished to leave this world of tossing waves, burnished sunlight and clean wet sand—but at last she flung herself towards a great wall of glassy green, letting the surging comber sweep her into the shallows. Then she splashed along the wet sand at the edge of the breakers, her dripping shirt and shorts clinging wetly around her. In the stiff sea breeze a brisk stroll to the end of the bay and around the point and she'd be dry again, at least she hoped so. She could imagine her sister's horrified expression. 'Liz! You

16

didn't arrive there looking like a drowned rat!'

A shadow fell across the water and she realised she wasn't alone on the beach. She swung around, startled, and a deeply-bronzed young man threw her a swift appraising grin as he splashed past in the shallows. Watching the tall figure in bright orange shirt and faded shorts as he moved swiftly ahead of her in the direction of a rocky point, she noticed he was carrying a 'kon-tiki', a diminutive fishing craft with a tiny sail and short baited lines. She could see no vehicle in sight other than her own and concluded he had come down on foot from the hills rising sheer from the black sand of the beach. A local farmer probably, judging by the mahogany tint of his skin so early in the summer season.

Funny how in that one instant the dark intelligent face had become so clearly imprinted on her mind. Strong features, soft dark hair ... but it was his expression that stayed with her ... contained yet vital, pulsing with life. If it hadn't been that she was finished with that sort of electric attraction she would have been alerted to this instant awareness of a stranger, run up a danger flag in her mind! As it was of course she was immune; what she felt about him was a matter of mere idle curiosity. Understandable really when you considered how few residents there were in this isolated coastal area. You couldn't help but take notice of anyone you met. Especially, an unexpected thought intruded itself in her musing, when the stranger chanced to be so undeniably attractive!

When she reached a rocky outcrop at the point of the bay where waves were dashing high in a cloud of spray in a gap between the rocks, she caught sight of him again. In a sheltered bay beyond the point, he stood in the foaming surf at the water's edge waiting as the breakers, aided by an offshore wind, carried the frail craft past the line of breaking surf and out towards the depths beyond. Two farm dogs waited on the sand.

Liz stood watching him launch his little kon-tiki raft. For some reason the stranger continued to hold her attention. Broad-shouldered, very erect, he was definitely worth looking at. Or was it merely the effect of a bronzed profile and vividly coloured orange shirt against a blue sea? At that moment he caught sight of her and lifted a hand to his forehead in a careless gesture of salute. Liz felt a shade of embarrassment in being caught out in staring so openly. She gave a hasty wave in return and turning aside, began to seek a foothold in the spray-swept rocks, from which she could leap across the gap to the opposite side.

'*Don't jump!*' The strong sea breeze whipped the words away, but she caught his shout faintly and paused, balancing herself with her back pressed against a high rock as she glanced towards him.

'Wait for me!' Abandoning his line, he hurried towards her with long purposeful strides. He was nearer to her now and she caught his words clearly. 'It's tricky crossing just there. There's a better place ... Hold on, I'll show you!'

'It's okay!' she called back above the thunder of an oncoming breaker surging towards her. She waited until the spray dashed over her and the wave ebbed away.

'*Don't try it!*'

Liz decided to ignore him. If this were a method of scraping up an acquaintance it was a new approach. If he were all that anxious not to lose sight of her all he need do was wait on the rocks on the opposite side. As for there being any possible danger in the jump across ... the windswept gap was certainly not a narrow one, but it wasn't too far for her to span in a leap from the cleft in the rocks where she stood. A wild sea was surging in through the opening, but if she chose the right moment to leap across ...

He had almost reached her when she braced herself, watching a wave ebbing away, dragging seaweed and sand in its wake. Now! For a moment she stood poised, then leaped towards a ledge in the rocks on the other side. Somehow, though, she missed her footing and all at once she was slipping, clutching wildly at the smooth surface, her fingernails scraping along the wet rocks, finding nothing to which to cling. Then she was falling to the jagged rocky surface below, conscious of a blow to her head. At the same moment a great wall of water thundered towards her to splinter in a shower of foam high above. She was tossed over and over, helpless as a rag doll, carried away by its force and submerged in a swirling sea. Frantically she tried to fight against the waves, to make her way to the surface. At last, gasping for air, she surfaced, but another comber swept in, dragging her with it, tossing her over and over, sucking her down ... down ... She was conscious of pain, of exploding red flashes, and after that she didn't have the strength to struggle any longer. It was easier to let herself slide helplessly into a tunnel of darkness that loomed ahead and towards which she felt herself being carried, faster, faster. Then there was utter blackness ... nothingness ...

She came back to consciousness slowly, vaguely aware of being in some shadowy place. Somewhere near at hand she could hear water dripping and around her rose the damp, fern-encrusted walls of a cave. A cave? But how could that be? And who was the man who was kneeling at her side? Even in this soft diffused light she was aware that he was watching her closely, appearing intensely relieved as she opened her eyes and fixed her glassy stare on his face. With wide dilated eyes she took in the strong features. 'What happened?'

Somehow his grin was infinitely reassuring. 'You slipped on the rocks over at the point, took a dive into the water when that king-sized wave swept you off the rocks and out to sea. I thought I was never going to catch up with you!'

'Oh.' For a moment she was content, wrapped in a sense of strength and security. In her dreamy state of mind she was satisfied to take his word for what had happened and why she was here, but another part of her mind insisted stubbornly on sorting things out. If only it wasn't all so hazy. She tried to raise herself to a sitting position, but his face wavered out of focus and she sank back into his arms.

'Take it easy.'

Bewildered, she put a hand to her forehead, conscious of soreness there, but swiftly he jerked her arm aside. 'Hey! Don't touch that! You don't want to start it up bleeding all over again!'

Mystification deepened in her mind. Don't touch what? A bandage, by the feel of it. Slowly, painstakingly, she was piecing the pieces together. When she'd last seen him, she told herself carefully, he had been wearing an orange shirt. Now the shirt was hanging open, one side roughly torn away, exposing a bare bronzed chest. So *she* was wearing *his* shirt, or a part of it. It was all very puzzling. Her head was beginning to ache and it was difficult to concentrate. 'I don't get it.'

'Don't try! You collected a gash on the head when you zoomed down on the rocks. Not much of a cut, but it bled a fair bit. There's always a strong rip out there at the gap. The rocks are slippery as hell and if you miss your footing when one of the big fellows come surging in over the rocks it can really put you in the drink! It's a risky jump at the best of times, worse from where you took off! That extra big wave swept you way out of my reach for a while ... thought I'd never catch up with you. I yelled out, tried to warn you not to take it on, but you'—his grin took the sting from the rebuke—'weren't having any. Guess you didn't hear me hollering with the wind blowing the other way.'

For once in her life Liz forbore to blurt out the truth, admit that she had imagined he had merely wished to scrape up an acquaintance with a girl on the beach. She was too intent on her thoughts.

'Feeling okay now?'

'Oh yes, yes!' To prove her words she jerked herself to a sitting position and found herself staring directly into the face of the man still kneeling at her side. For a moment she was struck by his eyes. A lively hazel, they seemed to be full of light. All at once unaccountably confused, she glanced away, said quickly: 'I remember now! That huge wave! I couldn't do a thing. It just sucked me down with it. Then you,' she finished thoughtfully, 'must have swum out and grabbed me. I——'

He waved aside her proffered thanks and getting to his feet stood looking down at her. 'Just happened that I was the one who chanced to be on the spot at the right time. Lucky really——' He broke off, a serious note tinging the vibrant tones. Liz remembered the expanse of wildly tossing sea and shivered. It had been a near thing, a brush with death, no matter how lightly he pretended to regard the sea rescue.

He misinterpreted her silence. 'I brought you in here to get away from the hot sun outside. You had a spot of concussion, but you weren't out for long after I caught up with you ... five minutes or so.'

He had lost no time in going to her help, she reflected. She owed him her life, yet somehow she couldn't seem to find the right words with which to thank him. She would make one more attempt, but this time she wouldn't look at him. There was something in his vital alive gaze that seemed to put everything else out of her mind. 'I guess I owe you——'

'Forget it!' His cheerful grin dispensed with the words that trembled on her lips. 'You could call it good practice! Out here on the Coast we have plenty of surf rescues in the season, but it's a bit early in the summer yet. You happen to be the first!'

She had a dim recollection of having passed a small building rising from a pile of rocks on her way along the beach. It must have been the Surf Life-Saving Clubhouse. To think she had been careful to swim only between the flags, and then to slip on those treacherous rocks! He was evidently a member of the local Surf Rescue team, a fact which no doubt explained his athletic appearance. He would need to be a powerful swimmer to battle against these rough seas. She brought her mind back to the deep tones. 'Is that your car and float over there on the grass under the trees?'

She nodded.

'Think you can make it that far?'

'But of course! I can easily walk back. I'm quite all

right now, honestly!' She leaped to her feet, but immediately the rock walls around her tilted alarmingly and she put out a hand to steady herself on the damp mossy surface.

'Okay, you've made your point.' She was aware of his searching glance. 'That does it. You'll have to travel the easy way. Quicker anyhow, and safer. I can't have you flaking out again.'

Before she realised what was happening he had stooped over her and she felt herself gathered, wet garments and all, in strong arms. Liz was so surprised she was speechless. Not that it would have made any difference, for what would be the use of arguing the matter with a man who was already carrying her towards the cave entrance and who obviously hadn't the slightest intention of doing anything else, no matter what she said to the contrary. He was infinitely gentle, holding her as effortlessly as though she were a child, his long easy strides taking them swiftly through the soft green gloom of the cave and out into a sudden blaze of sunshine. There was something disturbing yet oddly comforting in being held close against the sun-tanned chest. As he moved along the sands she stole an upwards glance at the strong dark face. He didn't *look* as though she were any great burden to him. Indeed, on the contrary he appeared to be enjoying all this. Suddenly he caught her glance and the firmly-cut lips twitched at the corners. 'What do I call you?'

'Me?' Hurriedly she collected her thoughts. 'Oh, I'm Elizabeth.' A glimmer of laughter lighted her eyes. 'But I usually answer to Liz.'

'Right, Liz. I'm Peter—Peter Farraday. Just over the sandbanks now and we'll be there.'

They passed the Surf Life-Saving Clubhouse, its high look-out affording an extensive view of the wide expanse of tossing sea and below, the stretch of beach where flags fluttered from tall poles. Then he was striding up the burning black sands of the sandhills and down the other side. Apparently the heated surface made no impression on his bare tanned feet, but no doubt, Liz mused, he was accustomed to the glittering ironsands.

When they reached the car he put her gently down on the long green grass beneath the trees. 'I'll be fine now,' she said quickly. 'Thanks for everything. Poor Red,' she glanced towards the chestnut, who was eyeing them enquiringly from the float, his long pale mane flying in the wind, 'he must have thought I was never coming back. *Never coming back.* She shivered as she realised how very close to the truth were the carelessly spoken words. 'Well,' she turned aside, 'I'd better be on my way.'

'Hold on.' He placed a hand firmly beneath her elbow, and she glanced up to meet those bright hazel eyes. There it was again, that intent look she found so difficult to meet. 'Travel bags, a horse and float ... planning to go much further today ... Liz?'

'Not really.'

'You're in no shape to drive a car, you know. Better let me run you up to the house. You can get into some dry gear, slap a bandage on that cut of yours. You're not in a mad rush to press on? There's no one you want to let know you'll be a bit late in arriving?'

She shook her head.

'Right! You're coming up to the house with me!'

All at once it seemed too much bother to argue the matter, and besides, he was already holding open the passenger door of the old car, settling her inside. A minute later he closed the door with a bang and slung his long tanned legs into the driver's seat. The two dogs suddenly appeared and came to join them, scrambling joyously into the rear seat among a jumble of cartons, boxes and horse gear.

She watched him in a bemused way as he put the car in gear and swinging across the grassy patch, ran along a short stretch of sandy roadway, then took a steeply winding road curving up into bush-clad hills. A battered jalopy with twin fins of surfboards rising from a roof rack swept past them on the narrow road and as the dust cleared, Liz realised they were moving along a well-worn track. Overhanging punga fronds and dust-coated spears of tall flax brushed the car as they went on. Tall tree ferns clustering around a wide entrance gate all but obscured a faded notice-board. *Arundel Station*. Beneath was a more recent notice: No Shooting.

Her companion got out to fling the gate wide, then returned to close it behind the car. Liz smiled gaily up at him. 'I always thought that was the passenger's job, opening and closing the gate?'

'You're excused today.'

They were taking a winding road that cut around the side of a cleared hill. Arum lilies grew wild on the grassy slopes and sheep scattered in mad panic at their approach. Presently there were two farther gates to be opened and closed behind them, two more notice-boards nailed to tree tunks. *No fires. No trespassing. Private road.* Liz raised enquiring dark eyes. 'Your property?'

'That's right.'

'You've put up an awful lot of notices, made your message loud and clear. Away out here in the country it's so quiet I shouldn't think—I mean, do you need them?'

'I need them.' At the sudden tightening of his jaw Liz did not pursue the subject. Glancing upwards towards a green-roofed timber house that sprawled against a backdrop of tall bluegums, she murmured lightly, 'You must be able to see for miles from up there on the hilltop!'

This time her remark evoked an entirely different reaction. The lean brown face was alight. 'It's one of the best views around. Up here we take in the whole sweep of the bay, can see right away down to the Heads.'

They rattled over a cattle-stop and took a curving driveway that led them past a loading ramp, the mellow red of shearing sheds, stock-pens, then they were sweeping past garages, taking a winding path bordered with drifts of pink, lilac and blue of massive flowering hydrangea bushes.

'Right, we're here!' He braked at the foot of a flight of worn timber steps leading up to a creeper-shaded verandah running the full width of the old colonial-style house. For a moment he sat motionless, well-shaped hands resting on the steering wheel, and Liz followed his gaze to the scene outspread below. She caught her breath. 'I can see what you mean by the view!' Far below was the incredible violet-blue of the Tasman, breakers creaming in wave after wave on a dark shore. A succession of bush-fringed bays fell away into the misty distance.

The next moment he was out of the car and the two dogs leaped down at his side. He reached for Liz's travel bag, then holding open the passenger door, eyed her closely. 'Feeling all right?'

'Oh yes, of course I am!' It was annoying and dismaying to realise she still suffered from the stupid dizziness. Not that she would admit such a thing to him! She had a dreadful suspicion that at the slightest sign of weakness he would scoop her up bodily once again, just as though she were a sheep ... or something ... and carry her up the steps. Fortunately the wave of weakness passed and pulling herself together she went up the steps at his side, hurrying to keep pace with his long easy strides.

They moved down a long passage until he threw open a door at the side, ushering her into a large airy lounge room with its worn carpet of indeterminate colouring, deep comfortable chairs and an old kauri table from an earlier era. Someone had covered the massive old settee with floral linen in cool shades of muted greens and turquoise and a massed flower arrangement standing on a low table gave evidence of a woman's touch. Liz couldn't understand her absurd sense of disappointment. She didn't know why she had taken it for granted he was unmarried simply because he had chanced to be alone when they met.

Crossing the big room, he leaned from a wide-open window and called to someone outside, 'Hey, Kate, are you around?

'No use.' Withdrawing a dark head from the opening, he turned towards Liz with a philosophical shrug. 'I may as well give up trying to get her. She's got this thing about gardening and now she's started on the vegetable plot down in the valley, she can't keep away from it. Won't be back for hours! Anyway, this is what you need ...' Moving towards a cocktail cabinet in a corner of the room, he poured a small glass of brandy and held it towards her. 'For you!'

'Must I?' She pulled a face but did as he asked—or rather *ordered*, she reflected ruefully. Nevertheless she had to admit that his suggestion had been a good one, for soon a warmth was stealing through her veins, banishing the last lingering remnants of weakness.

She reached up to place the empty goblet on the mantel, then stood transfixed as she caught sight of her reflection in the long-framed mirror overhead. What a mess she looked! A wet, bloodstained orange bandage around her head, scratched arms, torn fingernails, damp clothing encrusted with black sand. She only hoped the unseen Kate wouldn't make an appearance before Liz could escape from the house.

He seemed to read her thoughts. 'Your bag's over there in the room opposite,' he jerked his head towards an opening on the other side of the passage. 'Shower's down at the end,' he went on matter-of-factly. 'Why don't you dive in? It'll freshen you up, loosen that bandage too. You won't know yourself afterwards.'

'Well ...' Liz hesitated, aware of her grotesque appearance. Clinging dark sand all over her, smudged clown face with its orange headgear and dark bruising on her cheek. It would be heavenly to take a shower, but ...

He sent her a direct glance from alert hazel eyes. 'Kate would never forgive me if I let you go on without doing something about it.'

Kate. All at once she made up her mind. 'All right, then.' In the spacious, simply furnished bedroom with its heavy old-fashioned chest and twin beds, Liz took undergarments, shirt and jeans from her travel bag. The garments were worn and faded but blessedly sand-free and *dry*. Then, making her way along the passage to the bathroom, she was soon revelling in the cool shower that washed away sand from her hair and skin

26

and loosened the bloodstained bandage from her forehead. It was only a small cut after all, she realised now.

Presently she made her way back to the lounge room, a small, slim girl with enormous brown eyes in a face pale beneath the tan, damp dark hair combed and hanging free, a cool cream silk shirt falling loosely over faded blue jeans.

The man waiting by the window spun around to face her as she came into the room and Liz smiled up at him. 'Is this better?'

'Better? It's quite——' He broke off, a glint of amusement in his appreciative glance.

'A transformation?' Liz put in. 'Yes, I know.' No doubt she did look rather different from the dishevelled spectacle she had presented a short while previously.

'There's just one thing ...' Swiftly he crossed the room and reached towards a small box on the mantel. With deft tanned fingers he placed a small square of adhesive plaster over the cut on her forehead. He was very close, but surely, Liz told herself confusedly, that was no excuse for her intense *awareness* of him. Blame it on those brief moments of concussion.

'I've made coffee.' She turned away, realising there were two steaming pottery beakers standing on the big table. 'How do you like it? Black or white?'

'Black, please.'

'Good! That's how it is!'

She took the beaker he was extending towards her and went to perch on a low seat by the window. She couldn't help but wonder at the reaction of the absent, garden-loving Kate were she to return at this moment and find her husband entertaining a strange girl. Perhaps, though, folk who lived in this coastal area with its wild and dangerous surf beaches were accustomed to unexpected guests and sea rescues. Aloud she murmured: 'From up here you can see right down to the bay. There's a Surf Life-Saving Club look-out on the top of the rocks.'

He came to stand at her side, his gaze roving the

windswept sandhills and tossing sea far below. 'It's a terrific spot! Great for fishing too.'

'Fishing!' All at once she remembered the tiny kontiki raft he had been in the act of launching when she had reached the gap in the rocks. 'I hope I didn't spoil things for you today?'

'Not to worry. I usually leave the line out for a few hours. Later on I'll go down to the beach and see what the tide's brought in—going far?'

Liz realised that as yet she had given him no explanation as to where she was bound for or how she chanced to be swimming alone in a remote bay while nearby her chestnut waited in his float. All at once her face brightened, her husky voice was warm with enthusiasm as she glanced towards him. 'You'd never guess——'

'Tell me!'

'I've bought some property! It can't be far from here, and what do you know? I'm starting up a riding school for kids!'

'Riding? Not the old Rangiwahia block?' he cut in sharply.

'That's it! I'm the new owner.'

He didn't look at all impressed. On the contrary he appeared taken aback, wary all of a sudden. '*Bought it*, you said?'

'Why yes,' she faltered. 'What's wrong with a riding school anyway?'

He raised sardonic black brows. 'Nothing . . . yet.'

Liz decided to ignore his disagreeable attitude. After all, what she did with her money was no concern of his.

'I couldn't believe it,' she said warmly, hands cupped around the pottery beaker, eyes dreaming. 'You see, I'd been longing to go in for something like this for ages, but I simply didn't have the capital and the properties were all so expensive . . . way beyond anything I could ever afford. Then the most wonderful thing happened. I was left some money—not a great deal, but enough. I knew as soon as I saw this ad in the paper that it was just what I'd been looking for. Forty acres, it said, all in grass, with cottage . . . that means I'll have somewhere to live. Outbuildings . . . somewhere to keep the saddlery and all the rest of the gear I'll need. There's even a couple of ponies, and some riding gear. That'll be a start, anyway. "Suitable for riding school," the ad said.'

She glanced towards him, but he appeared more disapproving than ever. 'And you haven't seen the place before buying it?'

It wasn't so much what he said as the sardonic expression in his eyes that was so infuriating. All at once she couldn't endure his discouraging attitude one moment longer. 'No, I haven't!' She set down her empty beaker with a little clatter. 'You're just as bad as Helen!'

'Am I now?' He was merely amused by her outburst. 'And who's Helen?'

'My sister.' Liz's voice was taut. 'She's always raving on like that too, making difficulties, spoiling everything! Anyone would think,' she swept on hotly, 'that starting up a riding centre for kids was just about the most impossible thing anyone ever heard of. But I can manage it, and if Rangiwahia turns out to be anything like what I'm hoping it will——'

Peter Farraday sent her an unfathomable look, but merely murmured quietly, 'Well, you'll be able to see it for yourself pretty soon—cigarette?'

She shook her head. 'Not just now, thanks. I must get on. I just can't wait to see it!'

'Mind if I smoke?'

'Of course not.'

He flicked a lighter, held it to his cigarette and replaced the lighter in the pocket of the crisp white shirt. 'I'll run you over there.'

'Oh no, *please*—— I'm quite well again now. There's no need——'

'Just the same, I'll take you. You've taken one knock already today.' What he meant by that remark she couldn't imagine, although something about his wry grin was faintly disquieting. The protest she had been about to make died on her lips. Instead she asked, 'Is it far from here, the place?'

'No distance.' He waved his cigarette in the direction of the window and the sheep-dotted hills rising so near the house. 'Just over the hill. Bang next door to here, actually.'

'Really?' So he would be her nearest neighbour, this unpredictable man who in some strange manner managed both to annoy and attract her at the same time. She got to her feet, thankful to find that there was no longer any unsteadiness in her limbs. 'Do you think we could get along now?' Somehow she didn't want his wife to return and find her here. There would be endless explanations to be made and she had a growing conviction that the accident had been due to her own carelessness. Besides, she wanted to see her own land—and soon!

'Right! Let's go!' He crushed out his cigarette in a green glass ashtray. Liz hesitated, glancing back over her shoulder towards the glasses and stained beakers. 'How about those? Shall I——'

He waved a careless hand. 'Don't give them a thought. Kate'll fix them when she gets back.'

As they went down the verandah steps together Liz couldn't help but feel a sense of relief that she hadn't been forced into a meeting with the absent Kate. She might not ... she knew if *she* were his wife she wouldn't welcome... She brought herself up with a jerk, aghast at the direction in which her thoughts were leading her.

'But how will you get back?' she asked as he tossed her travel bag in the rear seat of the car and settled his long length in the driver's seat.

'It's no distance over the paddocks, when you know the short cuts!' He swung the car and float around in the driveway and presently they were retracing the route leading back to the main road.

'Do you run all sheep here?' she asked.

'At Arundel?' He nodded. 'That's right. I was brought up on a station; my folks are still over in the old homestead further up the coast. It was rough going when I first took the place over, covered in bush, overrun with gorse and blackberry, but I'm breaking it in gradually. Cleared away the bush for a start, except in the dips betweeen the hills.' Liz's gaze moved to the patches of burnished green running up the gullies. Clusters of tall forest trees, kauri, tawa, rimu, rose above thickly-growing pungas and lacy tree ferns. She brought her mind back to the deep vibrant tones. 'Helicopters do a tremendous job when it comes to spraying gorse and blackberry, and you can't beat the top-dressing boys with their light aircraft when it comes to ringing in the hill country.'

'You work it on your own?'

'I've got a couple of lads with me. They help out and get a line on how to do the job at the same time. There goes one of them now!' In the distance Liz discerned a motor-cycle hurtling at a precipitous angle down a grassy hillside, followed by two sheepdogs. 'Wayne likes his "mountain goat" to chase around the boundary fences, but Tim, he's like me. He prefers the horse every time for hilly country—I guess that's something you'd understand.' He lifted his gaze to the small mirror overhead with its reflection of the horse-float behind them. 'Is he a show-jumper?'

'Is he ever?' As always when she spoke of Red, Liz's small face was alive with interest. 'Red's won oodles of ribbons. Do you know once, just once, at a big country show, he won the purple ribbon for Champion Hack! I've never felt so proud! Only,' the eager tones fell a little, 'I haven't shown him or hunted him for the last two seasons. It was so difficult living in town and grazing Red miles away in an outer suburb, and what with working at the hospital and having odd hours . . .' Her voice trailed away. It wasn't true. It was because of Leon that she had given up the outdoor activities she loved. He had had no time for horses or riding. And where had all the sacrifices got her? Just nowhere at all! Catch her ever again putting aside her own interests merely to please a man! Aloud she said: 'I'm just longing to get Red settled in alongside where I'm living instead of having him twenty miles away!'

As the last gate was closed behind them she realised

they had left Arundel station behind them and were taking a winding, bush-fringed road. It seemed only a short distance and they were turning off the main highway, running in towards an opening in a long boundary fence of macrocarpa pines.

Liz turned a surprised face towards him. 'But this isn't—Rangiwahia?'

'It is, you know.' He was skirting a taranaki gate of barbed wire and light batons lying in the long grass at the entrance.

'It can't be ... I mean, I didn't expect it to be ... like this!'

CHAPTER 2

PETER FARRADAY made no answer and as they bumped over the rutted ground Liz gazed in growing consternation at the rough paddocks over which they were travelling. Ahead she could see a red-roofed timber cottage, clearly in dire need of painting and repair. As they turned in at an open gateway and sped down an overgrown pathway between trailing roses and giant overhanging shrubs, the picture became even less prepossessing. The area of lawn surrounding the buildings had been recently trimmed, but the cottage was a dismal-looking dwelling with flaking white paintwork and rotting front steps. A short distance down the broken pathway stood a huge empty shed, doors swinging open and sagging on their hinges. Could that derelict-looking place be the barn mentioned in the advertisement? she wondered wildly as the car slid to a stop.

'The view,' Liz clutched at the single aspect of the property that appeared to match up to her glowing expectations, 'is really fantastic! Almost the same as the one you have from your home——' She stopped short. Imagine comparing *his* well-stocked thousand-acre station with *her* rough paddocks! Ignoring his lack of response, she struggled determinedly on. 'One thing, there's oodles of grass everywhere. Long grass too.'

It seemed, however, that he had no intention of letting her off one thing. 'Always is at this time of the year.'

Suddenly a question sprang into her mind, something she should have considered first of all instead of now, when it was probably too late. 'Fences?' Her gaze swept the flat green paddocks around her. 'I wonder——?'

His shrug was ironic. 'What fences?'

It was, she realised, all too true. A few short lengths of boundary fences remained intact, but the greater part consisted of sagging posts and rusted, trailing wires. There were gaps where stock had pushed their way through, or broken through more likely, for what was there to prevent them? Now she realised why the taranaki gate at the entrance to the property had been left lying in the grass. Open or shut, what difference did it make? She made a final effort to rally her swiftly fading hopes. 'The horses . . . I caught a glimpse of them just now. They were grazing at the back of the big shed down there. Perhaps . . .'

He shot her one of those swift sardonic glances and she found herself regretting having allowed him to bring her here. If only she could have faced her moment of truth alone! In a flash she had leapt from the car and slammed the door behind her. Then she was hurrying down the overgrown pathway, pushing aside long sprays of pink rambler roses that clutched at her with their thorny tendrils. Uninvited, unwelcome, he caught up with her and strolled along at her side, but she no longer cared. All she knew was that she might as well find out the worst and get it over with. Passing the derelict shed, she glanced inside, but the dim recess appeared to be empty, except for a few cracked and rotting bridles hanging from a peg on the rough wall, a bulging sack standing in a corner.

When she reached the back of the building the two ponies grazing nearby raised their heads to gaze at her with lack-lustre eyes. They were both quite old, she realised at once. One, a piebald, evidently accustomed to being fed bread or carrots, moved towards her with an expectant air and limping gait. Liz stooped over to lift a small hoof, placing an exploratory hand over a hard swelling on the fetlock.

'It's no use trying to do anything about it,' Peter told her. 'It's a permanent injury.'

He was right, of course, damnably, horribly right—as usual! Unconsciously she sighed and turned towards the bay pony who came trotting towards her. He had, she realised, a definite sway-back, and it was clear that neither pony would be of the slightest use to her. Absently she stroked two soft muzzles.

The perceptive hazel eyes that seemed to see so much more than she would like were fixed on her despondent face. 'Not quite what you expected, hmm?'

'Not quite.' She tried to keep her voice steady.

'I did try to warn you.'

Liz didn't answer. He seemed to make a habit of warning her, she reflected crossly, and all to no purpose. First of all the rocks, then Rangiwahia. Not that it made the slightest difference—she made an effort to control her trembling lips—for today she seemed bent on collecting trouble for herself.

'It sure could do with a spot of doing up. Well,' he spun around on his heel, 'I'll go and get your chestnut out of the float. He must be about browned off with it by this time. All right if I put him down here with the ponies?'

'Yes, of course.' What did it matter? she thought wildly, as he left her to stride towards the car. What did anything matter today?

When the horse had been let loose to explore his new surroundings, Liz gazed towards a large closed shed not far from the cottage. 'I wonder what's in there? We might as well go and take a look.' Together they moved up the broken pathway.

As Peter flung open the double doors a large rectangular area sprang to view. The big, high-ceilinged room was dim and shadowy in contrast with the bright sunlight outside, but as her eyes became accustomed to the gloom Liz discerned a long table beneath a window. A telephone stood on the table and she moved towards it. It wasn't surprising to find the line wasn't connected. At least, though, the barn-like place appeared to have been recently built and was of more solid construction than the ramshackle old shed down the yard. Her gaze slid around the unlined walls, the emptiness. 'Whatever could it have been meant for originally?'

'The first owners of the place ran a poultry farm.

They had this built for use as a broody shed,' he told her.

A broody shed! She had a wild impulse towards hysteria.

'Hello there! I didn't hear the car arrive or I'd have been out there to welcome you!' A tall angular woman of middle age wearing a sleeveless floral frock stood in the open doorway, her short wiry grey hair outlined in a nimbus of light. 'You'll be Miss Kennedy, the new owner?' The tanned face broke into a pleasant smile. 'We were wondering, Stan and I, whether you'd get here before dark.'

Liz nodded. 'That's me, and you're——?'

Another wide and friendly smile. 'We're the Gallaghers, Evelyn and Stan. We heard the cottage was empty and moved in last month. But there's plenty of room,' she added quickly. 'Come along inside. Stan's somewhere around. I'll go and find him.'

There was no need, for at that moment a stockily-built man in his early sixties with muscular shoulders and grizzled grey hair strolled towards them. He extended a toil-roughened hand towards Liz.

'Stan's been a bushman most of his life,' his wife explained, 'but he's given it up now and we thought we'd take a holiday for a few months while we look around for something easier he can do. Meantime,' even in the midst of her crushing sense of disappointment Liz was aware of the anxious note in the clear tones, the silent appeal in the grey eyes, 'would it suit you if we stayed on for a while? We'd pay the usual rent for the cottage, of course.'

'Evvie's a first-rate cook,' her husband offered with a shy grin.

'And he's ever so handy at fixing things around the place,' his wife put in, laughing.

'I don't see why not.' Somehow Liz couldn't seem to think straight. Everything she had found here had turned out to be so different from the perfect riding-school set-up she had envisaged. 'You're both welcome to stay meantime. Afterwards,' she sighed, 'well, I'm not sure yet what my plans are.'

'That's good enough for us,' Evelyn said on a note of relief. 'Now come inside and I'll show you around the place. We've only been here a short while ourselves, but if we stay on we could do the rooms up a bit. Stan's a dab hand when it comes to painting and paperhanging, and the cottage is simply crying out for some work to be done on it——' She turned towards the tall man standing silently in the background. 'How about you, Peter? Are you coming along to the cottage too?'

'Thanks, Mrs. Gallagher, but I won't join you this time. I've got to get cracking.' His gaze lingered on Liz's wan face with its dark bruising on the cheekbone, and a hint of concern coloured his tones. 'Have an early night, Liz. Time enough to worry about things in the morning.'

'I suppose so.' She turned dispiritedly away, a sick feeling of disappointment welling up within her. She had been so certain that everything here would match up to her dream picture, and now . . . Oh, for those shining white fences, prancing ponies, the well-stocked barn with its saddles and bridles neatly arranged on their brackets! The dilapidated old shed was large enough for use as a barn, goodness knows. Large—and empty. Bare of saddlery, feed, gear, of everything she had hoped to find there. The inner fences on the property were practically useless as they stood, or rather didn't stand, she told herself ruefully. And as to the horses . . .

Peter's vibrant tones broke in on her despairing thoughts. 'Think about it tomorrow. And look, if you get the slightest sign of anything wrong, headache, blackout, *anything*, just give me a ring at Arundel and I'll be over right away with the doc.' He turned towards the other two. 'Liz took a fall out on the rocks today, over at the Gap. Collected a spot of concussion.'

'Oh, that's too bad—but don't worry,' Evelyn Gallagher said in her deep quiet tones, 'we'll keep an eye on her.'

'Right! I'll get back. See you!' A lift of a bronzed hand and he had turned away, to vault a low fence and go striding away across the paddocks.

'Wait!' Liz was out of breath when she finally caught up with the waiting figure. 'I just wanted to say ... well, thanks for everything! And will you tell your wife,' she rushed on in her soft husky voice, 'that I'm awfully sorry about all that sand I left on the carpet——'

'My—wife?' For a moment he eyed her with a puzzled stare, then his expression cleared. 'You mean Kate? She's not quite in my age group. Aunts never are, do you think?' The lively hazel eyes glinted with a teasing light. 'I'll tell you something, though, Liz.' He threw a backward grin over his shoulder. 'When I find my own special kind of girl, you'll be the first to know!'

Liz went back over the paddock in a turmoil of emotion. She didn't know what to make of him. That boob she'd made mistaking him for a married man ... anyone could have made the same blunder. There was no need for him to make such a ... a thing of it! Maddening to remember how deeply she was indebted to him. She owed him her life, no use trying to get around it. She had been knocked unconscious by a blow to the head—thoughtfully she fingered the swelling on her forehead—and but for his swift action she would have drowned out there on the sunlit beach.

'I couldn't help hearing what you said.' She became aware of Evelyn strolling towards her. 'That Kate, she's a relative of Peter Farraday who housekeeps for him and the two boys working on the station. Not that they'll be needing her there much longer, from what folks are saying around here.' They climbed through the sagging fence and approached the cottage. 'Stan and I used to live in this district a few years ago and at that time Peter was in love with a local girl, Beryl Manning her name is now. Her parents were alive then. They owned a huge sheep station not far away. Then quite suddenly there was some sort of quarrel. No one knew what had really happened, but Beryl rushed away to Queensland and after a while we heard she'd married a grazier there, a widower with a young

38

son. Darryl his name is, and they say she dotes on him just as though he were her own. Beryl only came back here for a visit, but they tell me she's been here for months now, staying with Darryl and her aunt Olga up at the old homestead. And now that Beryl's free——'

'Free?' Liz was well aware she was encouraging a gossip session, but she couldn't seem to help herself.

'Oh, didn't I tell you? Her husband died just a few months ago. He was years older than she was and he took a sudden heart attack. One thing, she'll have no financial worries. They say her husband was awfully wealthy and she was well off even before she married him. No property problems either. The manager who had been looking after the station since her parents died left a month ago, but she sent to Australia for a new man and he's living now in the farm cottage on the property. Beryl's come back looking lovelier than ever, though I simply can't imagine how that could be! I always thought of her as the most beautiful girl I ever saw. I caught sight of her again just the other day and she's exactly the same—— Oh, she's not young any more,' she ran on in answer to the surprised expression in Liz's dark eyes, 'but she *looks* young, and that's all that matters. Not the sort of girl a man could forget in a hurry. Heaven only knows what brought her back to this little corner of the world, a girl like that who could live in any capital of Europe if she wanted to. *Or what keeps her here now*,' she added significantly. 'She always said she hated living in the country, she made no secret of it, yet now she doesn't seem to think of leaving.'

'Maybe she has friends in the district?'

Evelyn shook her cropped grey hair back from her face. 'Beryl was never one for girl friends and all the men she used to know around here are married now ... except Peter. Oh well, she's the sort who always manages to get her own way in the end. Good luck to her.' Reflectively she chewed a long blade of grass. 'He looks you so straight in the eye it's hard to believe what happened a while ago between Peter and the last owner of this place, but from what Lance Pritchard's parents told us——'

'Come into the cottage and have a look around!' Stan had come to join them and the three went up the rickety steps together. Soon they were moving through a tiny dark hall into a sparsely furnished living room. 'The picture from the windows makes up for a lot!' Stan jerked aside the long faded velvet curtains and a vista of sea and bush-clad hills and far bays sprang to view. Somehow, though, Liz was having difficulty in concentrating on anything in the cottage. Her thoughts kept reverting to that disturbing Peter Farraday. Not married yet, apparently, but it wouldn't be long. So he had already found 'his own special kind of girl', although why it should matter so much to her was something she failed to understand. Something else too nagged below the surface of her mind. What had Evelyn Gallagher meant by her reference to some sort of disagreement between Peter Farraday and the previous owner of the property?

'There's a nice big kitchen.' She became aware of Evelyn's friendly tones as they moved into another room. 'And the electric range cooks well, even if it is an old model. Stan says if we're staying here for a while he'll put in a stainless steel sink bench. He's got one stashed away in the shed—these are the bedrooms.' The rooms were spacious and airy, the floors covered in worn cheap linoleum, dressing chests and beds in need of a fresh coat of paint. In the front bedroom her worn travel bag lay on the tidily-made bed. On the worn bureau a glass vase held a single Shot Silk rosebud.

Evelyn thrust aside a hanging curtain in a corner, exposing a line of hooks and hangers in a makeshift wardrobe. 'It looks a lot worse from the outside than it really is. There's nothing really wrong with the place.'

'No.' But there was a lot wrong with her own private little world—so much so that she could see no way out of her difficulties. Later, seated with the Gallaghers at the small round table covered in gay floral cloth, Liz picked listlessly at the tastefully prepared meal of salad and cold meats as her mind went over and over the situation. She wouldn't give up right at the outset.' There *must* be a way of surmounting the unexpected financial hurdle if only she could think of it.

'How much would it cost to replace the fencing?' she enquired suddenly.

'How much?' Stan put down his knife and fork while he considered the matter. 'Well now, you'd have to get a contractor in to do the job. Mind you,' the rich thoughtful tones flowed on, 'the boundary ones are good enough for a year or two yet and a lot of the others could be patched up to last a long time. Were you thinking of running stock on the place?'

Liz nodded. 'I thought ponies ... about fifteen. A sort of riding school was what I had in mind.'

'I see. Well, horses would take a lot less wiring to keep them in than sheep would. Guess you could count on a thousand dollars at the very least.'

A thousand dollars! For all the difference it would make to her state of finances it might just as well be ten thousand. She realised the other two were eyeing her curiously. Stan said: 'You planning to get the place fixed up right away?'

'No.' Liz's head was bent, dark curtains of hair falling around her face as absently she traced a pattern with her fork on the tablecloth. 'Just thinking.' After a moment she glanced up. 'You know, I got the idea from the solicitor when I bought the property here that the last owner had ideas along the same lines, but he couldn't have done much about it. There's no gear about the place—well, none that's any good at all; no horses except those two pathetic old ponies down in the yard; no proper fencing inside the boundaries. What happened? Did he change his mind?'

'He had it changed for him——' Evelyn said. 'He would have stayed longer, but——'

Her husband sent her a warning glance. 'He wasn't the type for country life. We only met him once, just as he was moving out, but anyone could see he wouldn't be interested in that sort of set-up. Seems his father set him up here, hoping Lance would give it a go as a riding place, but it was all just a waste of money so far as he was concerned. He had a holiday here and so did his friends from town, but as to making a living out of the place——' He threw up weathered palms. 'I believe at the beginning he did have a small amount of riding gear, a few hacks and a couple of decent ponies —his parents saw to that—but that was as far as it went. He didn't even take the trouble to fix up the fencing. Guess he'd never tackled that sort of work, a city bloke like him——'

'Or any sort of work either, if you ask me!' Evelyn's husband silenced her with a significant glance that wasn't lost on Liz.

When the tea things had been cleared away she arranged her clothing in the bureau drawers that jammed each time she opened them. With her radiogram and records standing in a corner of the living room, her personal belongings scattered around the bedroom, the cottage took on a slightly more homely air. The Gallaghers, after assuring her they would be on hand if she needed them, retired early, and soon Liz too prepared for an early night. Not, she told herself, because *he* had suggested it but merely because there seemed little else to do.

Picking up a novel, she settled herself comfortably against the pillows and attempted to read, but the printed letters danced beneath the light from the naked bulb overhead as more pressing matters clamoured for her attention. 'Leave it till morning,' Peter Farraday had told her. Sound advice, if she could follow it. Switching off the light, she closed her eyes, but she felt too strung-up to sleep. She lay listening to the unfamiliar sounds breaking the intense stillness of the country. The mournful 'more-pork' of a native owl somewhere in the bush-filled gully below, the dull roar of the surf. Yet she must have drifted off into slumber, for some time later she found herself hazily wondering where she was. Recollection came rushing back and at the same moment she became aware of a sound that alerted her to instant atttention, the soft pad-pad of footsteps passing on the path below her window.

Slipping from bed, she went to the window and parting the windows, peered outside. Could that be a man's shadow moving towards the barn at the end of the path? Not that it would do him any good if burglary was his aim, she thought wryly. Perhaps she had imagined the moving shadow, but just to make certain ... Throwing a filmy brunch coat over her shortie pyjamas, she caught up a torch and moving down the dark little hall, let herself quietly out of the door and out into the moon-silvered night. As she hurried down the path she collided with a tall figure emerging from the cave of blackness that was the open shed and without stopping to think she pressed the switch of her flashlight. Immediately a man's startled face sprang to view, a thin young face with a shock of tousled blond hair and a fair beard, eyes wide with apprehension.

'You scared the wits out of me! Put that thing out, will you?'

'You scared *me*!' Liz realised the gangling figure wore dark jersey and slacks, rubber-soled shoes. A sack dangled from his hand. 'What have you got in there?' she cried sharply.

'Hold on!' He put the sack down on the pathway between them. 'I can guess what's on your mind, but you've got it all wrong! I just nipped back for something I left behind in the barn the other day when I lit out—— Hey!' The flashlight that Liz held in her hand wavered over the narrow features. 'Now I get it! You're the girl who bought me out!'

'That's right.' Liz was feeling more and more bewildered. 'Now I'm going to ask *you* something! Why all the secrecy? You could have come back here any time. I'd have given you whatever it is you want——' All at once a thought flashed through her mind. She had been told by the solicitor that there had been a certain amount of gear left at the cottage and included in the sale of the property. Was he——?

'Saw the lights were all out, didn't want to wake anyone up,' he muttered. 'It was just some personal stuff, clothing and all that,' he went on evasively. 'What was the idea of buying this place anyhow?

43

Thinking of an investment?'

'I haven't decided . . . yet.'

'Well, take my advice and don't ever go in for running a riding school. Believe me, I know what I'm talking about! It doesn't work out—not with Farraday living bang over the hill. He's forced me out of the place and he'll do the same for you if you try anything in that line.'

'You did start a riding school, then?'

'I had a crack at it. Half a dozen nags, a bit of gear, that was about it. I was going to go in for more horses, more gear, but hell, what was the use? The fences were in a mess and Farraday went crazy if stock got into his territory. In the end I decided to call it a day, thanks to Farraday, I got rid of the lot. He wasn't satisfied until he'd queered my pitch, sent me packing.'

'But he couldn't *force* you to go.'

'You reckon? I'll tell you what he can do! He can make life so damned unpleasant for you that it isn't worth the effort trying to make a go of it! Do you know what happens if one of your nags happens to stray over the boundary into his precious hillsides? He threatens you with legal action! Once he pointed a gun, scared all hell out of me! How was I to know I'd made a mistake and was on his land instead of my own? Take it from me, you'll never get anywhere with him around. He's forced me to opt out and he'll do the same for you!' An ugly sneer twisted the slack lips. 'But I got my own back on him! I kept my mouth shut about getting out of here, waited until he was well out of the way down South, then I shoved a For Sale ad in the city papers. I knew he'd never see it. The next week I got a sale for the place, thanks to you!'

She switched off the flashlight. 'But I don't understand. Are you trying to tell me that this little property could possibly mean a thing to a big landowner like Peter Farraday?'

'It could mean a lot! I happen to know that he's mad keen to get hold of it.'

'With all the acres he owns?' They were speaking in whispers. 'I can't believe it. Why would he——'

44

'Can't you guess? This place happens to have easy access down to the beach. All it needs is a track bulldozed through the bush. Besides, there's something else that's a lot more important in these hot dry summers, and that's a good water supply from the creek down there in the gully——' He stopped short, staring down at her, and all at once his voice was hoarse, ingratiating. 'Hey, you look mighty appealing in that get-up. Can't think why I didn't notice before.' He took a step towards her. 'What are we doing, wasting time?' Before she could guess at his intention he had caught her in lean arms and was crushing her roughly against his chest. Liz struggled violently, pushing against him with both hands.

'Get out!' Her muffled cry cut through the silence of the night and at the same moment a shadow, darker than the rest, advanced swiftly towards them. A businesslike fist shot out to land squarely on a bearded chin and the youth crumpled and fell to the ground. The next minute he was on his feet, shaking with fury. 'What's the big idea? I wasn't doing any harm!'

'What were you hanging around here for, then?' Even in the dim light, Liz could see Peter's threatening expression.

'Nothing, nothing!' The youth fingered a bruised jaw. 'Can't a guy come back to collect his own property?'

'So that's it!' In a swift movement Peter bent, spilling the contents of the sack out on to the pathway. A gleaming saddle, obviously new, a jingling bridle, a silver-mounted whip. '*Your* property!' Peter's voice was cutting. 'You knew these went with the sale of the place. Thought you'd get away with it, just as you did with the rest of the gear! It's not your stuff and you know it!'

'Give me——' The whining tones died into silence as Peter took a menacing step towards him.

'Get out of here, Pritchard, *fast*, or I'll see that you do!'

'My dad's whip, it's got his name on it . . .'

'Take it!' Peter flung the whip after the cringing

figure, 'and get moving! If ever I catch you hanging around here again you'll be sorry. Get it?'

'Okay, okay, I'm going!' Mumbling something under his breath, he scuttled away and in a few moments the sound of a motor revving up came clearly to the two standing on the driveway.

'I thought he was up to something.' Peter's expression remained grim. 'I happened to be passing and saw his bus standing at the gate.'

Liz knew she owed him some thanks for his timely intervention, yet somehow the words stuck in her throat. Illogically she felt angry with him. In some queer way she *had* to be angry with him, otherwise ... 'You needn't have *hurt* him!'

'He deserved a lot more than that! Sneaking back here, making off with your property, making a nuisance of himself. One thing, you have no need to worry about Lance Pritchard. He won't be back.'

'No.' She wasn't particularly concerned with the previous owner of the place. It was the man at her side who mattered. The thoughts tumbled wildly through her brain. Come to think of it, she had good reason for any antipathy she felt towards him. The other prospective buyer for the property, could it have been one Peter Farraday? If so, if he still coveted Rangiwahia, how gratified he must be at her obvious disenchantment with her purchase. Was that the reason he had insisted on escorting her here today, in order to witness her disillusionment? He had only to play a waiting game and before long she would be pleased to pass the property on to him. Was that what he was counting on?

'Why didn't you tell me about what happened to the last owner here when he had ideas of starting up a riding school, instead of letting me rave on about it? All the time,' her husky tones rose indignantly, 'you must have been laughing at me!'

'Just what did he tell you,' his voice was dangerously quiet, 'about me?'

'He said you threw him out of the place——'

'That's not true. He——'

'Well, as good as.' She shrugged slim shoulders. 'He

46

said you made things so darned unpleasant for him he was forced to go. He told me——'

'And did he tell you,' his tone was low, contained, 'that he and his mates from the city had a merry old time shooting wild duck and pheasant out of season, over my land? That gates were always left open, valuable stock killed on the road by fast cars, ewes frightened, fences broken? One night I happened to see some tractor lights over in the paddocks, caught Pritchard and his gang out there with guns and magnetic torches. I sent them on their way in a hurry! It wasn't until the morning that I came across my stallion,' his voice deepened. 'A great horse, one of the best. He'd been so badly injured with a rifle shot that I had no choice but to finish the job. *He* said they'd been shooting 'possums in the trees, that it was an accident.'

'No,' Liz whispered, 'he didn't tell me . . . all that.'

'I thought not. Now look, Liz,' his tone lightened, 'I didn't let you in on all this before because I didn't think for one moment that you'd give the idea a thought, not when once you got a line on what the place is really like. That is, not unless you've got a heck of a lot of cash stashed away to spend on doing it up!' He sent her a keen look. 'Have you?'

'No,' she whispered despondently.

'Pity. It would help.'

'I bet that pleases you a lot!' She couldn't seem to stem the words that came tumbling from her lips. 'The solicitor told me there was someone else interested in the place and Lance Pritchard said that because of the creek you wanted the property here for yourself——'

'That's right.' His tone was deceptively casual. 'I'm still in the market. Interested?'

It took a moment for the significance of what he had said to register. 'You mean, will I hand it over, to you?'

'Well, will you?' He spoke so quietly yet she had an impression that he was waiting expectantly. 'You won't get any other bids if you put it back on the market and you won't lose by my offer, I promise you.'

Liz knew she should consider the opportunity to rid herself of a purchase that promised her nothing but

47

worry and frustration. Maybe if the offer had come from anyone else she might have decided right now to call it a day, but to hand it over to the owner of Arundel station, the stranger who one way and another had already become all too much involved in her affairs . . .

'No!' She drew a deep breath, contrived a shaky smile. 'I guess I'm a bad loser. I'm just not giving up without a struggle. I'll think of something,' she added wildly, not knowing how the miracle was to be achieved. 'I'm not sure what yet, but—something!'

'Just as you say. It's up to you, and don't forget that if you change your mind, the offer still stands.'

Forget. She only wished she could. Trouble was, there was something about *him* she couldn't put out of her mind. Tall, tanned, vibrantly alive, already he seemed a part of her life. Liz pulled her thoughts together and attempted to sound businesslike.

'Now say I manage to get the place fixed up,' her attempt at nonchalance fled before his mocking look and she glanced away. 'Just say I do—well, you won't need to worry about the ponies being any trouble to you. I mean, they'll have to be quiet and not too young for crippled kids to be safe on them——'

'*What's* that you said?' He was staring down at her incredulously.

'Spastic children,' she explained patiently. 'Oh, didn't I tell you?' She went on to describe in detail the project that meant so much to her. 'But I've just had an idea,' she lifted thoughtful dark eyes. 'I've got a little capital left and if I could get a couple of paddocks fenced off then I could look around for some ponies and secondhand gear. It would be a start, even if it meant taking a few children at a time. Is there a contractor around these parts? Someone who would do the job in a hurry?'

If he were disappointed at losing his chance of acquiring the land with its plentiful water supply, he concealed it well. 'Sure there is. I'll get in touch with Charlie first thing tomorrow. He'll get on to it right away.'

'Thank you. Ask him to send the account to me, please.'

'I'll tell you something,' Peter said, 'there's a horse sale coming up at Omera, a few miles from here, next Friday. I'm hoping to pick up a stallion there so, if you'd care to come along just to have a look——'

It was scarcely a warmly-worded invitation, but then they hadn't been exactly friendly during the last few minutes. Anyway, what did it matter? The thing was to get her project launched as quickly as possible.

'All right, then.' She tried to match his cool tone. 'Who knows? I may even come back with a few ponies myself!'

'Pick you up around nine, then.'

There was a little silence. A round fat moon over-head emerged from a blanket of cloud and flooded the lawns with silver, softening the outlines of the ramshackle buildings. The cool night wind that was whipping Liz's garments around her slender body tossed a strand of dark hair across the man's face. Swiftly she jerked her head aside. She glanced up and meeting that dark and brilliant gaze, for a heart-stopping moment she wondered if he were about to kiss her.

' 'Night, Liz.' Abruptly he turned and moved into the shadows of the driveway. Liz stood where he had left her. She felt almost ... disappointed ... until she remembered about 'his own special kind of girl' and took a firm hold of her runaway thoughts. And only just in time, she told herself a moment later, as a feminine laugh echoed out of the darkness. Somehow it hadn't occurred to her that Peter might not have been alone when he stopped at her gate. 'But, honey,' a voice childishly high and sweet with an unchildlike note of intimacy, reached her clearly, 'what kept you so long? I thought you were never coming back.' Slowly Liz moved back towards the cottage. There was no reason why he shouldn't be with Beryl. Beryl, who had everything.

Back in bed once again she went over the events of the long day and suddenly the old tempestuous spirit rose in her. All she needed to make a success of her venture was some spirit, a little organisation—and a lot of luck! What if there were fences to be renewed, horses to be bought—she'd manage, just, if she started in a small way. It would of course mean a short-term venture, six months instead of a year, but once she got the scheme under way and could prove it to be a success, others might be interested and willing to carry on. And she *would* get it started, for this wasn't just in her own interests, this was something involving a lot of kids who otherwise would never ever know what it was to feel high above others, instead of being eternally low in their wheelchairs. To enjoy, just for a while, a place in the sun! It was her one chance and she refused to allow anything to beat her, right at the outset. A challenge, but—all at once she came face to face with the truth—was her interest entirely selfless? Could it be that her stubborn determination to stay and make a go of things had a lot to do with proving herself to that strangely disturbing Peter Farraday?

CHAPTER 3

ON the following morning a truck piled with fencing materials drew up in the driveway and a middle-aged man with bare tanned chest and shabby khaki shorts asked to see the owner of the cottage. If his eyes betrayed surprise at Liz's youthful appearance he said nothing of his thought but swiftly got down to business and soon they were strolling over the paddocks discussing the costs of labour and materials.

By the end of the day the work was completed and as the dust-coated truck moved away, Liz was formulating plans. If she bought three ponies and a few second-hand saddles and bridles at the horse sale, at least it would be a beginning.

During the course of the following few days she found herself kept frantically busy owing to the continuous ringing of the telephone at the cottage. It all began when Stan enquired of a farmer friend in the district who happened to have two saddles for sale at a low price. On learning of the purpose for which the saddles were intended, however, he refused to make any charge, throwing in a number of used bridles for good measure. In the manner of news in country districts, word travelled swiftly on the grapevine regarding Liz's needs, and soon other farmers were following the example. Cars, trucks and Land-Rovers pulled up on the broken driveway and soon a mounting pile of saddles and bridles, horse-covers and gear littered the floor of the old shed.

One evening Liz answered the telephone to a male voice who told her he was speaking from a farmhouse a few miles distant. Stafford was the name. He'd just heard of Liz's worthwhile venture for the handicapped kids and if she could make use of a couple of ponies

51

that his own lads had outgrown . . . ? He could guaran-
tee them to be sound, quiet, good-natured, and if she'd
cure to take them both he'd send them over in the
morning with one of the boys. Liz was delighted with
the offer and thanked him warmly.

The 'boy', when he appeared on the following
morning at the wheel of a big cattle truck, was a dark-
eyed young man, very tall and thin, with a slow manner of speaking and a pleasant smile. As Liz went to
meet him he was unloading a black and white pony
from the truck and for a moment he seemed to have
difficulty in wrenching his gaze from her excited face.
'But they're just what I want,' she cried delightedly.
'What are their names?'

'He's Silver——'

'I could have guessed that.'

'And this fellow's called Little Joe.'

'And you're——'

'Malcolm.' A dull brick colour was creeping under
the tan of his cheeks. Liz thought: He's shy of girls.
He's more at home with horses. To help him out she
moved towards the truck, picked up a fleecy white
sheepskin. 'Don't tell me you're giving these away too,
and the saddles, and all the gear?'

He nodded. 'Dad threw it all in.' He eyed the
ponies, standing docilely at his side. 'They're pretty
overweight, could do with some exercise. If you like,'
he offered eagerly, 'we could take them for a run
down to the beach and see how they go?'

'I'd like that? Come on, we'll saddle them up and
try them out!' Liz stooped to pick up a bridle and
fitted it in the mouth of the small white pony, then
threw a sheepskin over his back. As stirrup leathers
were lengthened and harness adjusted she reflected
that both mounts appeared quiet enough to be
trusted to stand perfectly still while small disabled
riders were lifted up on to saddles.

'You know something?' She turned a laughing face
back towards Malcolm as they set off on a narrow path
that led down to the gully below. 'I haven't even been
down this track to the beach yet!' Her own mount had

a jerky action, but she couldn't help thinking that Malcolm appeared even more uncomfortable as he bumped along behind her, his long legs hanging incongruously at the sides of the black pony.

Presently they moved into the filtered green light of native bush. Branches of great evergreen trees met high overhead and the ponies had to step over fallen punga-logs lying on the damp leaf mould underfoot. A peal of bell-like notes broke the intense silence and looking upwards Liz discerned, high on a branch of towering puriri tree, a tui's white throat and black plumage. At her side she caught the sheen of water among overhanging bush and thickly growing ferns. The creek was larger than she had expected. Thinking of the creek, however, made her mind revert to Peter Farraday, whom she had already allowed to intrude far too much into her life and her imaginings. Swiftly she wrenched her thoughts aside.

Quite suddenly they emerged into the sunshine. Pulling up her mount, Liz looked down the steep bush-covered hillside to the wide expanse of diamond-bright black sands below. She was forced to cling to a coarse white mane as the pony's short steps took her down the twisting crumbling cliff path dropping sheerly to the beach. They reached the sand at last and their mounts sluggishly responded as they were urged into a trot, then an uneven canter, the hoofs leaving a line of small indentations on gleaming wet sand.

All at once a helicopter came into view, dropping low over the sea as it followed a line of tossing breakers. Someone waved from above and the two riders on the beach pulled rein. Malcolm's gaze went to the ponies, already breathless, their shaggy coats wet with sweat. 'They need exercise, these two, that's for sure!'

But Liz's eyes were raised to the helicopter cruising above the white surf. 'He waved to us,' she said in surprise.

'Who? Oh,' Malcolm squinted up into the sun, 'that would be Peter Farraday.'

'For goodness' sake!' Liz continued to eye the

'copter in wonderment. 'What would he be doing up there?'

'It's a safety patrol chopper,' Malcolm's voice was careless, 'just part of the Surf Life-Saving programme. Peter's quite a guy in that line. Got his Life-Saving Bronze Medal, captain of the local club, and was in a team competing for the world championships a year or so ago. He's well known around these parts as a champion swimmer.'

'Yes, I know.' How she came to know of Peter's life-saving technique she didn't explain. Somehow she didn't want to remember all that she owed him; how very much in his debt she happened to be.

She pulled on Silver's bridle. 'Race you back to the track!' Now there was no reluctance on the part of the ponies to hasten their pace. They cantered along the beach, flew up the dry sand and were soon scrambling up the crumbling cliff path.

When they arrived back at the cottage Liz slipped from the saddle. As they rubbed down their sweating mounts Malcolm turned on her an enquiring dark-eyed gaze. 'Well, what do you think of them, Miss Kennedy?'

'It's Liz,' she smiled across at him, 'and they'll do me just fine! They're both exactly the type of ponies I've been thinking of for the children. A bit sluggish, maybe, but exercise will soon put that right. What I like about them is that they stop and start obediently and they don't jump at an unexpected sound. A pony that leaps at something that zooms up out of the blue wouldn't be any use at all. I was so pleased when the helicopter skimmed over just above them. All that noise, yet neither Silver nor Little Joe turned a hair.'

'Good.' He was still regarding her with a puzzled stare. 'But if the kids are handicapped with their legs no use to them, won't you have to fix up the gear a bit to suit?'

'Oh, I've got lots of ideas about that! I've been working on it for ages! This isn't something I've dreamed up in a minute, you know! I've got it all figured out. Safety stirrups are a must, and the same goes for neck straps to help the children learn to balance on the horse's back. But the main thing is a belt with leather handles. It goes around the rider's waist and means the helper can hold on and keep him steady. Know the sort of thing I mean? Wait, I'll show you!' She went to the big open shed and after a moment returned and extended towards him a special safety belt.

'Tremendous!' Malcolm inspected the belt, then eyed her with a grin. 'You really are wrapped up in this project of yours, aren't you?'

She laughed, 'I really am.' Then her voice sobered. You would be too if ever you'd worked among kids like that.'

'I guess. Look, could you use any help? I mean, anything at all?'

'Could I ever? I've got oodles of things waiting to be fixed up before the children come out for a ride next week. Stan's awfully good, he's over there now sorting out timber to make a wheelchair ramp and when that's done he's promised to put up a long railing we can hitch the ponies to. But if you could give me a hand to fix up the gear ... there's such a lot to be done.' She hesitated. 'But can you spare the time? I mean, how about your own work on the farm?'

He grinned. 'I'm a tiger for good works! Especially when it happens to be over in this direction! And it's not like you think. I'm anything but indispensable over home. My brother Philip, he's the one who's crazy about farming and country life, but it's not for me. Engineering's more in my line. I'm off to university in town at the start of the new term. Meantime I'm a sort of dogsbody around the place, at least at home that seems to be the general idea. My time's my own,' he grinned cheerfully, 'and yours! I'm all for project Liz Kennedy!'

They spent the afternoon seated on the grass outside the cottage, sorting out piles of neck-straps, safety belts and riding caps. 'I've got the special irons made for the stirrups,' Liz told him, 'but they'll all have to be changed over. Not that I'll be able to take many children for a start, but we can get the gear fixed up, even if there are only half a dozen riders at the beginning. Then maybe, after a while . . .' Her eyes were wistful, her hands idle on the leather stirrup she was unbuckling as she stared unseeingly over the unkempt grounds.

'Gee, it's really something, what you're taking on.' She brought her mind back to Malcolm's heartfelt tones. 'I bet there aren't many girls as pretty as——'

Liz laughed and wrinkled her nose. 'There aren't many girls who have a chance with working with handicapped kids, getting to know them——'

'But to go to all this trouble and expense——'

'No trouble! I'm enjoying it.' In spite of herself she sighed. 'It's just . . . well, I'm a bit short of funds at the moment.'

The young boyish face wore a puzzled frown. 'But you can't mean you're trying to do this all off your own bat? Isn't there something, anyone else to help, financially I mean?'

Liz shrugged and tightened a rusted buckle on a leather strap. 'There's a fund being set up where the public can send donations for special equipment, improvement to the grounds and all that, but so far it hasn't really got going.' Her usual buoyant spirits asserted themselves. 'But once I can get some advertising started, when people really get to know what I'm trying to do——' She tested a rusted buckle. 'Everything just has to be *safe*, that's the thing! It's all been done before, you know, I've read about it, but not so far in this country. I want the children to have proper lessons,' the warm eager tones ran on, 'learn to ride as well as they can with the special gear, play ordinary gymkhana games, egg and spoon races, bending—all on horseback.'

'I get it,' Malcolm said. 'Treat 'em the same as if they were ordinary kids learning to ride.'

'That's the idea. Well, I'm on my way, and with a bit of luck——'

Luck, it seemed, was already heading her way, for the following morning when she went out to the mailbox nailed to the rickety front gate, she found a type-written letter awaiting her. What was even more important, it contained a cheque. Her eyes widened as she stared down at the slip of paper. It was unbelievable, it was too good to be true, but it was! A cheque to the value of one thousand dollars! An accompanying letter from the Fund-Raising Committee of the Riding School for the Disabled informed her that the donation had come from an Auckland firm of solicitors whose client preferred to remain anonymous. The donation was for the purpose of purchasing ponies or buying special equipment needed for the school or making improvements to the existing grounds.

She ran down the path, waving the cheque towards Stan who was busy with hammer and nails as he worked on the timber ramp he was constructing. Malcolm, who had appeared early in the day, was helping the older man in his task.

'Look! It's just arrived in the mail! And guess what? It's a thousand dollars! A donation! Now we can get the whole place fenced into paddocks, I can buy more ponies, really get going——'

'And I thought,' Malcolm groaned, 'that I was finished with sorting out horse gear and mending halters——'

'How about me?' complained Stan. 'This means I'll have to get cracking on making a corral as soon as I've finished the timber ramp.' His creased, weather-roughened face, however, betrayed an expression of satisfaction that matched Liz's look of excitement.

'Not to worry,' Malcolm told him, 'just call on me any old time at all and I'll give you a hand!'

They were both so kind, Liz reflected gratefully. Indeed, everyone in the district had been helpful—except Peter Farraday! Apart from his off-handed offer to escort her to the horse sale, and he intended going there himself in any event, he had made no offer of assistance towards her project. But then—how could she have forgotten—it was scarcely in his interests to further her schemes, hare-brained and impracticable as he no doubt thought them. She could scarcely wait to tell him her news! The thought of her victory over him made her sing happily to herself as she moved towards the barn, now converted into a recreation room for the small riders. A dresser held cold drinks and glasses, and a coffee percolator and beakers were arranged on a table beside an electric point, for the convenience of helpers and parents. The children could eat their lunches while seated at the big table and on a wet day the barn would prove ideal for wheelchairs. Evelyn had discovered some long forms for seating and Malcolm had driven up one morning with an old honky-tonk piano that he and Stan had lifted down from the cattle truck and placed in one corner of the big room. A door at the end of the barn led surprisingly to a small washroom and now that the place had been cleaned and dusted it was a definite asset. The telephone connection had been renewed, and that too was an excellent arrangement. Liz went inside and dialled the home number of the fencing contractor, who by a lucky chance was there. Yes, he would come back right away, he could get the job finished by the end of next week. Liz was feeling so pleased at the unexpected stroke of good fortune that she rang the Cerebral Palsy Institute then and there.

How was she making out at Rangiwahia? the superintendent enquired with interest.

'Oh, everything was going along fine!' Liz's husky tones rang with enthusiasm. She could be ready for the children's first lesson by the end of next week, so if arrangements could be made for them to be transported by ambulances to the riding school ...? By organising two separate parties, one to ride in the morning, one in the afternoon, she could accommodate quite a few riders. She'd expect them with the doctors and therapists on Friday then?

Her mind was running ahead excitedly. She'd get more ponies tomorrow and then, glory be! In a few days she'd be away! Wonderful to think that tomorrow when Peter arrived to take her to the horse sale she would go there not as a mere onlooker as he anticipated, but as a definite buyer! *She had the money,* now that she had no need to spend her entire capital on fencing the place. And won't *that* make your black eyebrows rise, Mr. Peter Farraday!

The cluster of dust-coated vehicles on the country road left no doubt in Liz's mind that they were nearing the saleyards. The next moment pens and stockyard swept into view against a backdrop of fenced green paddocks. Peter manoeuvred the big cattle truck in a space between a stock truck and trailer and a late model car, and soon they were making their way through the crowd of young and old who had come to look and perhaps to buy. Liz was aware of a blending of smells compounded of horse, dried grasses, hay, as they moved towards the pens.

'Hey, Boss!' Peter swung around as two youths of about seventeen years pushed a way through the throng in her direction. Wearing light shirts and faded blue hipster jeans, they were deeply tanned and obviously worked out of doors. The short youth with freckles and red hair, and the slight dark one, were both eyeing Liz, neat and trim in her white shorts and sleeveless striped tan-and-white shirt, tan sneakers on her feet.

'Liz Kennedy—this is Wayne ... Tim. Liz is here on business.'

Two sinewy young arms shot out as the boys continued to gaze appreciatively towards Liz, smiling and animated, her great brown eyes glimmering with her own secret triumph.

'That's right.' She giggled. 'I'm playing the stock market—just for today! We're on our way to have a look at the ponies.'

'But ...' Wayne's round freckled face expressed bewilderment. 'Not the one who's running the new riding outfit over at Rangiwahia? You can't be,' he finished slowly.

Liz laughed, 'I am, you know. Why, what did you expect me to look like?'

'*He* said——' Wayne swung hotly towards his mate. 'Why did you say she was fiftyish if she was a day?

Horsey type, you told me, and bossy as they come!'

'Aw, gee,' the slim youth squirmed uncomfortably. 'I was only having you on,' he muttered. 'How was I to know she'd look like that—sorry, gotta go!' He turned abruptly and escaped among the milling crowd.

'Well, anyway,' Liz couldn't help but be amused at Wayne's obvious embarrassment, 'why don't you come on over and see what the place is like for yourself? I'm hoping to get the school really started on Friday.'

'Thanks, Miss Kennedy, and if there's anything we can do to help, Just sing out.'

'I'll do that.'

She threw a smile over her shoulder as Peter, an arm placed beneath her elbow, swept her away and they made their way through the groups. The women and girls looked cool and attractive in their gay cotton shifts, the men wore shorts and shirts featuring vivid flower and sea motifs of the neighbouring Pacific islands. All wore rubber thongs on bare brown feet.

Peter appeared to know the greater proportion of the farmers who had come to the horse sale, but he merely lifted a hand in salutation as other men hailed him or sent a friendly grin towards an acquaintance. Liz was unaware of heads turning to glance towards the tall, broad-shouldered young station owner and the slim dark girl whose head barely reached his shoulder.

Presently they reached the pens where the horses waited, each stamped with a number. Liz's gaze ran along the pens where the sun gleamed on shining coats of chestnut, grey black, of hunters and hacks. A half-broken colt with rolling eyes restlessly circled his pen. Liz paused beside an enclosure where three foals stood close together, far from the mothers they would never see again. 'If only...' she sighed. 'Today I've got to keep my mind on ponies. What I need is something over five years yet not too old or unsound. You know?'

'You've made up your mind to get a couple today, then?' His tone was quite off-hand as though the subject scarcely interested him. But he'd be interested enough in a minute, Liz mused with secret glee, when she told him ... Deliberately she dropped her gaze, fearful he might surprise the triumph that danced in her eyes. She made her voice match his careless tones. 'I thought maybe if the right sort turned up, I'd pick up half a dozen or so while we're here.'

'Wow!' His low whistle of surprise was infinitely gratifying. 'Just as well I brought you along today!'

'Oh well,' she caressed a woolly-coated foal who was pushing against the pen, 'it makes a difference having the place fully fenced. It means I can get going with the classes sooner than I thought I could. Next week, actually.'

'Good for you, Liz!' Glancing up, she didn't quite know what to make of the quizzical expression in his hazel eyes ... or the silence. She wouldn't be surprised if he weren't deliberately withholding the question she had been angling for. In the end she was forced to enlighten him. 'I suppose you're wondering what happened to make me change my mind since I saw you at the cottage that day?'

'What did make it happen, Liz?' His voice was unexpectedly gentle. 'Another legacy? Some of that luck you wanted land on you after all?'

'Oh yes, yes!' Her face was alight with excitement. 'Something fantastic happened! You see, this cheque from the solicitor arrived in the mailbox. Someone in town had made a donation to the fund. The moment it arrived I knew I could carry on with getting the fencing done. The contractor has promised me he'll have it finished by next week. And since I've seen you a farmer around here, a Mr. Stafford, gave me two ponies his family had grown out of, and that meant I could buy half a dozen more with the cash I had in hand,' she ran on a trifle incoherently. 'So,' she smiled gaily up at him, 'here I am!'

'I see. Well, after that,' he took her arm and began to pilot her through the throng, 'we'd better check on the ponies.' It was at that moment that something happened to Liz, something entirely unexpected. A wild excitement fluttered along her nerves and she was flooded by a sort of in-depth happiness. The green and gold day? Fulfilment of a dream? Which dream, Liz, the riding school for the disabled? Or this man at her side, his bronzed hand resting on her bare arm? Why do you feel that you could go on for ever like this, Just the two of you, alone amid the crowd? What makes you wish the day would never end?

They had paused beside the pens with their shaggy ponies. 'Which one of these takes your fancy, Liz?' Peter's matter-of-fact tones, his enquiring sideways glance, jerked her back to reality.

Still fighting that bemusing sense of happiness, she gestured towards the pony nearest to her, a small plump piebald. 'He doesn't look too young or inexperienced ... doesn't seem as though he'd have any bad habits. What would you say—Peter?' The name came strangely to her lips. Absurd to feel this sudden self-consciousness about a name, merely because it was *his*.

'Not that fellow, Liz! Not in a hundred years!'

'He looks okay to me.'

'Maybe, if you don't happen to know him! That chap's got a nasty little habit of kicking up his heels at the slightest excuse. He'd toss a kid off his back in no time at all!'

'This one, then? He looks quiet enough.' She moved towards a small bay pony who stood with half-closed eyes, drowsing in the sunshine.

Peter shook his head. 'I know her too. They can't keep her weight down and she founders quite a lot. For my money,' he ran his eyes along the line of ponies, 'this one is a good buy, and this bloke, and the one at the end of the row. The little black mare too. I'd say they're a sound enough bunch,' he pronounced a few moments later when they had inspected the selected ones.

'What I like about them,' Liz said thoughtfully, 'is that they're so quiet. I mean, if they can take all this hullabaloo without getting excited——'

'You've got something there.' He was writing numbers down on the back of a cigarette packet and she came to peer over his shoulder. 'Number eleven?' She was surprised. 'You don't mean that skinny little grey with the dull coat and the don't care look about him? He looked to me as though there was something wrong with him.'

He grinned. 'Nothing that a few good feeds won't put right. I happen to know where he comes from,' his tone hardened, 'and it's an outfit that shouldn't be allowed the care of animals. You can take it from me, Liz, he's a great little pony, just the ticket for those special kids of yours. You won't ever be sorry about having Cobber as one of the gang.'

'Cobber! That's a nice friendly little name.'

'He's a nice friendly little bloke! Nothing of the odd-bod about him, believe me——'

'I believe you.' She smiled towards him and as their glance met and held, once again Liz felt herself shaken by that surge of wild, sweet happiness. Almost like ... love. With an effort she brought her mind back to the matter in hand. 'I'll ... take him.'

All at once a thought occurred to her. 'How about the stallion you were thinking of buying?'

He shook his head. 'There's nothing outstanding here. Not one to match the one I lost. Looks like things are moving. Let's get up on the stand, shall we?'

They climbed up on a bench on the makeshift stand and took a seat between a family party and two brawny Maori farm workers.

In a high box the auctioneer overlooked the crowd and as a broadly smiling Maori man led in a black and white cattle dog the auctioneer launched into an amusing patter. The cattle dog went to a young farmer and a wire-haired terrier was led into the yard.

'I'd love to buy him,' Liz whispered. 'He keeps looking right at me and he's awfully hard to resist, but I've got a dog already. At least, Evelyn's promised to get one from a friend of hers. What I really need is a goat, a nice tame one I can christen McGinty.' At his glance of surprise she ran on, 'I have to have lots of smaller animals than the horses, ones the children can play with while they're waiting for their turn to take a ride. They'll be useful too, so the ponies won't be startled or

frightened of strange noises or sudden movements——
She broke off, staring down into the yard below. 'He's
going to sell some gear. This I must see!'

Bidding eagerly in her soft voice, Liz presently
found herself the owner of a dozen used bridles and a
number of worn but well-cared-for saddles, still in
sound condition.

The assistant rushed around the yard as the first
horse entered the enclosure, a bucking stallion ridden
by a Maori youth in a gay pink shirt and denim jeans.
There was a crack of a stockwhip, a wild 'Yahoo' as
horse and rider approached the jump and sailed over
the rails. The hunters were brought in next, followed
by the yearlings. Then a man came into the yard leading a sturdy stock pony and Liz leaned over to consult
the numbers Peter had jotted down on his cigarette
packet. 'Will you do the bidding? The auctioneer can
hear you a lot better than me, and you know what I'm
wanting.'

'Leave it to me.' It seemed that for the first time in
their brief acquaintance they were in complete agreement. Certainly she had confidence in his judgment.
He had helped her to choose the ponies, he understood
the type of temperaments she wanted in the mounts,
and she felt he would offer a fair price but no more
than they were worth.

The bids came slowly for the ponies and one after
another was knocked down to the couple on the centre
stand. Presently the auctioneer blew his whistle and
the sixth pony was disposed of to the same bidder.
'Knocked down to the man in the top row and his
lady!' the auctioneer told the crowd, and all eyes
moved towards Peter and Liz. She wanted to cry out
and tell them all that of course she wasn't 'his lady'.
They were here together on a mere matter of business.
Are you sure? Deep down a tiny voice plucked at her
mind. *Are you certain that's all there is to it?*

They waited a little longer, watched the transfer of
the woolly foals and high-spirited yearlings, then Peter
turned towards her enquiringly. 'Had enough? Shall
we make a move now?'

She nodded. 'If you like.' She was feeling so happy and excited she didn't much care what they did, so long as they were together. That, she scolded herself the next moment, was what success did to her. Went to her head and made her feel quite lightheaded.

Peter arranged with the officials that he would pick up the ponies in an hour's time, then they were strolling along the dusty path towards the waiting vehicles. She was so lucky, she mused, in Peter having brought a big cattle truck to the sale, even though he had probably expected to take back only a stallion; maybe a pony on her behalf.

'Where are we going?' she asked as the truck moved off along the quiet country road.

'Just to get a spot of lunch, if you're interested?'

'Oh, I am! I'm so thirsty! All that heat and dust——'

'And bidding!'

'You did most of that!'

He sent her a swift glance, deep and intent. 'Happy, Liz?'

'Am I?' She laughed her throaty laugh on one note, gazing out of the window at the sweeping green paddocks with their grazing beef cattle. 'I should be,' she added contentedly. 'I'm really on my way now. The ambulances are bringing the children out next week for their first riding lesson——'

'It's not going to be a matter of kids just having a bit of fun, then?'

'It is not! They're going to get a new look at life, those kids, complete mobility, and they're going to be taught to ride the right way.' She laughed up at him. 'Weekly riding lessons with all the thrills but not the spills! You wouldn't believe,' all at once her enthusiastic tones were touched with feeling, 'the mental anguish of kids who can just never get around except in wheelchairs or on crutches. It'll mean a lot more to them, the lessons on horseback, then just strengthening muscles.' Her eyes were thoughtful.

'You mean, the psychological benefit!'

She nodded eagerly. 'You wouldn't believe what it's

going to do for them. Can you imagine what it must be like to have to slither around the floor like a fish? And then this one thing, this one step that will spur them on to others! It's funny, but riding seems to relax the muscles that react so violently to any other ways of making them respond——' She broke off, adding after a moment of silence, 'I guess I get carried away sometimes, but it means such a lot. It's more than just giving them a sense of achievement——'

'A new dimension in life?'

'That's it! I'm even hoping——' Her voice died away. It seemed such an ambitious scheme for one person to hope to achieve.

'What are you hoping, Liz?'

'Oh, just that some day in the future, it could be turned into a national centre of riding for the disabled. A place where helpers and instructors all over the country could gather for classes and courses. You know?'

'Why not?' He appeared unsurprised at her grand schemes, or maybe he was merely not interested. 'You don't mind all the work?'

She shook her head. 'When it's giving the kids so much pleasure I get a lot out of it too. Sounds corny, I guess, but that's the way it is.'

'And you're planning to do all this on your own?' Nothing could be more casual than his careless enquiry.

'Oh yes. You see there's only me.'

'No male friends around to give you a hand with things?'

'Well, there'll be the ambulance drivers, they're marvellous really. Some of the doctors who work along the same lines are interested, and I'm hoping a few of the fathers will care enough to come along as helpers——'

'That,' he said drily, 'wasn't quite what I had in mind.'

'Oh, you mean boy-friends? I haven't any,' Liz said cheerfully. With a little shock of surprise she realised that Leon had scarcely entered her mind since her arrival at Rangiwahia. It must have been because there had been so many other matters to fill her thoughts.

They swung around a corner and entered a street where a handful of old-fashioned shops were scattered along the main road. A sign outside a small timber building said: 'Teas. Lunches.' Peter pulled up beneath a shady tree growing by the footpath and escorted Liz through the open doorway and towards a table under a wide-open window, where the wind blew refreshingly cool and fresh on their hot faces. Lunch was a simple affair consisting of freshly-cut sandwiches and cups of steaming hot coffee. Afterwards Peter lighted her cigarette and one for himself and they sat talking, the blue smoke rising companionably between them.

'So you're all set to go next week, Liz?'

She nodded and ran on in her impetuous way, 'I can hardly wait to try out these new ponies we got today! I'll have to start thinking of names for them. How does——' She stopped short, staring in surprise towards the tall, quite startlingly beautiful blonde girl who had entered the room. Liz was so astonished at the sight of anyone so incredibly lovely, wearing such eye-catching fashion garments, in this tiny tea-room at the back of beyond that it wasn't for a moment she realised the girl was threading her way between the tables in their direction. Her walk was the unhurried stroll of one who takes attention as her due.

All at once Liz had no need to ask who the stranger was. Who could it be but Beryl? The happiness that had coloured the day faded like a rainbow in the mist. In that one brief glance she had taken in flawless features, short-cropped silver-gilt hair. Cool and poised, fresh as a shower of summer rain, the other girl made Liz miserably conscious of her own dust-smeared hands and grubby white shorts.

'Peter!' The vision paused beside them, laid a proprietorial hand on the man's tanned arm.

He rose to his long length. 'Hello! You two girls had better get to know each other. Beryl, this is Liz.'

For a fraction of a second pale frozen blue eyes moved towards Liz. 'Oh yes, I heard you were living in the old cottage down the road.' She made it sound, Liz thought indignantly, as though she had taken up residence in a slum.

'I thought you'd taken off for the weekend,' Peter was saying.

'Oh, come on,' pink iridescent lips pouted teasingly, 'can't a girl change her mind once in a while?'

Liz was struck by the high, little-girl tone that contrasted so sharply with the older girl's sophisticated appearance. The same voice, she realised now, that had reached her out of the darkness a few nights previously. She brought her mind back to the light tones.

'Sandy thought we might pick up something at the sale for Darryl. He's got this thing about wanting to ride horses all of a sudden. Goodness knows why, unless it's through watching too many cowboy serials on television. Anyway, I thought a pony might be a better idea to start him off with, so we came over to the saleyards today to have a look. Trouble was we struck car trouble—Sandy's down at the garage now having the car checked by a mechanic—and by the time we got to the sale all the ponies had gone. We saw your truck parked outside. I should have let you know I was going.' Her tone implied that had Peter known Beryl too was attending the sale he would of course have dropped all such trifling matters as Liz Kennedy and her schemes for a riding centre and taken Beryl instead. 'Did you pick up a stallion?' She contrived to entirely exclude Liz from the conversation.

'No,' Peter crushed out his cigarette in the ashtray on the table. 'Actually Liz was the one who was doing all the bidding at the sale.'

'So I heard.' With one flick of her sweeping lashes the other girl dismissed all Liz's grand schemes. She felt as though she weren't here at all, but the next moment she told herself that she refused to allow herself to be relegated to nothingness.

'That's right,' she said brightly. 'I bought six ponies! Now I'm longing to get them home to see how they turn out. They're for the children——'

'Oh,' Beryl murmured contemptuously, 'kids.'

Evelyn had been right about this girl, Liz mused hotly. She was certainly accustomed to having things all her own way. If this was all the eye-catching loveliness did for one—— Jealousy, jealousy, she chided herself.

'Here comes Sandy now,' Beryl said, and Liz turned to see a fair-haired stocky man in his late thirties advancing towards them. As she smiled up into Sandy McPhail's rugged features Liz found herself taking an immediate liking to this open-faced man with the honest grey eyes and firm hand-clasp.

'I've been hearing things about you, Miss Kennedy,' there was a suggestion of a Scottish burr in the forceful tones. 'That's a great effort you're putting on over at Rangiwahia.'

'Thank you,' Liz felt a warmth stealing around her heart, 'but I'm really just beginning——'

'Sorry, Pete,' the high imperious tones cut across Liz's husky voice, 'but we can't stay. Sandy's got this appointment back at the house with a stock agent.'

The manager of her property, however, appeared in no hurry to leave. 'Let him wait!'

'No, we'd better go!' Beryl flashed her brilliant smile in Peter's direction. There was an intimate note in her voice. 'See you tonight, Pete.'

Liz's gaze moved to the tall figure, but his gaze was inscrutable. ' 'Bye. See you, Sandy!'

A vague nod in the direction of Liz's flushed face and Beryl had turned aside, leaving behind her a faint fragrance of Blue Grass perfume and so far as Liz was concerned, a definite sense of deflation.

Mingling with her tumultuous feelings was a wave of sympathy towards the station manager. Imagine being in the employ of Beryl Manning! How could a strong, self-reliant type of man such as Sandy McPhail appeared to be ever have put himself in such an invidious position? Especially since he had known Beryl before coming to the district and must be well aware of her demanding ways. There would be no lack of employment offering for a man of his capabilities and experience. It was difficult to understand why he stayed, unless ... Was he too under the spell of that cool blue gaze? She wouldn't wonder. Peter and Sandy! It wasn't *fair*. Her thoughts went off at a tangent. Odd, the haunting sense of familiarity she felt about the other girl. It was unlikely they had ever met. That was another thing about which Evelyn had been quite correct in her assessment, she reflected wryly. The blonde elegance of the other girl was something one simply couldn't forget!

'We'll have to be getting back too.' All at once the shining sunshiny day had lost a little of its peculiar magic. It was only a shabby little tea-room after all, dull painted walls, fly-speckled pictures on the wall, and it *was* growing late. She gathered up her suede shoulder-bag, got to her feet. 'Shall we go?'

While Peter paid at the counter she strolled out to the truck and soon they were driving back in the direction of the saleyards.

When they reached the yards the crowd was dispersing and the Land-Rovers, trucks and trailers jammed the narrow road. Liz waited in the cab while Peter went to fetch the ponies and load them into the truck. The sun had slid behind a billowing mass of gunmetal cloud and the breeze was whipping up little puffs of dust in the roadway. All at once she was in a hurry to get away from here and back to the cottage. There was so much to be done in preparation for the opening of the riding school next week. Besides, keeping herself busy prevented her from thinking too much of ridiculous things like her and Peter Farraday becoming friends in spite of the turbulent beginnings of their acquaintance. Just for a while, back there on the stand, she'd had a warm contented feeling ... found herself liking him ... quite a lot. Somehow she'd got the impression that he felt the same way about her, but of course it was only an illusion.

Soon they had left the tangle of vehicles behind and were sweeping between vast grazing paddocks and out towards the bush-clad hills of the coast.

Liz couldn't understand why she felt so dispirited, as if the day hadn't been so successful after all. Just the usual country horse sale. Nothing special about it. In spite of her purchase of the ponies, somehow she could think of nothing but Beryl, cool and poised, perfectly in control of the situation. *'See you tonight, Pete!'*

CHAPTER 4

Liz was up very early on the day on which she expected the disabled children, accompanied by medical experts and therapists, to arrive from the city. She was strolling over the long grass, her bare feet brushed with heavy drops of dew when she became aware that someone else had arrived here still earlier. A moment later she recognised the two station hands from Arundel. Wayne's red head was bent as with a hoofpick he probed the lifted hoof of a piebald and Tim was busy brushing the shaggy coat of a bay pony. Both youths glanced up as Liz hurried over the grass towards them. 'It's awfully good of you to come over here, but you shouldn't have bothered.'

'No bother, Miss Kennedy!' Tim paused, brush in hand. 'We like it over here. Can't think why, though. Can you, Wayne?'

She smiled up at two sun-darkened young faces. 'It's Liz, you know——'

'He'll feel a whole lot more comfortable with those stones out of the way,' Wayne put down the pony's small hoof. 'We knew you'd be flat out this morning getting ready for that wheelchair invasion of yours. The boss said to tell you——'

'Never mind that.' Impatiently she brushed aside Peter's anticipated advice as to how she should run her venture. This was *her* day and she was quite capable of seeing it through without his instructions or interference in her plans. 'Tell me,' she went on quickly, 'what do you think of the ponies?'

'Seem sound enough from what we can see of them.' Apparently Tim, the slight dark youth, did the talking for both. 'They'd be a pretty dumb bunch for ordinary riders, I guess, but for the sort of set-up you've got in mind, you need them as quiet as they come.'

'That's the idea,' she agreed, 'just so long as they're good-tempered and can be depended on to stand still while we get the children mounted. That's the main thing—— Hey! Wait your turn!' For ponies were converging on her from all directions, crowding around her as with tossing heads and seeking muzzles they competed for the carrots she was taking from a scarlet plastic bucket.

'How many kids are you expecting today?' asked Tim.

'Twenty-seven—that is, if they all turn up.'

'Good on you! Just tell us what you want done and we'll get stuck in!'

'Everything's under control, I think—no, wait!' A hand flew guiltily to her mouth. 'I meant to get one of the drinking troughs shifted up near the ramp. Never mind, there's an old washing machine bowl up there and a tap, and if we could run a piece of plastic hosing into it for water——'

'Leave it to us, Liz. It's as good as done! Operation Kennedy!' The two lads, with their farming backgrounds, appeared to know exactly what was needed. Ponies were caught and led into the tea-tree corral; gates opened in readiness for the ambulances to pass through.

'They'll have the doctors and physiotherapists with them this first day,' Liz told them, 'so that the experts can get an idea how the children will go, if it's safe ... all that sort of thing. It's a sort of try-out really. Heavens!' she glanced down at her wrist-watch, 'I'll have to fly! They'll be here before I know where I am!' She hesitated. 'Would you boys like to come in and have some breakfast with us?'

'We'd like it a lot, Liz,' once again it was Tim who answered, 'but we've got to get back. So if you're sure there's nothing else we can do for you——'

'I'm sure, and thank you.' They strolled back towards the cottage together, then the boys got into their battered jalopy, waving a cheerful goodbye as the vehicle, belching clouds of smoke from the exhaust, turned into the driveway.

It had been a thoughtful gesture on the part of the boys, Liz mused, appearing at the cottage to help her this morning. Not like 'the boss' who hadn't even troubled to give her a ring on the phone to wish her luck today. Not that she expected any word from him, of course, but it would have been ... well ... neighbourly. She wished—Liz took herself sternly in hand and shaking the traitorous thought away, went inside to a breakfast which after all she found herself too strung-up to eat.

When she returned to the yard she found a gleaming scarlet sports car standing in the driveway and Malcolm leaped out. 'Hi, Liz! Thought you might be glad of some help, seeing it's your big day?'

'Oh, I am! I am!' She was delighted to see him. 'If you could saddle up a few ponies, tie them to the hitching rail all ready for when the children arrive——'

'Say no more!' he grinned cheerfully. 'It's as good as done! Just what I was going to start on anyway!' He went whistling down the path and a few moments later emerged from the open shed, bridles jingling over a bare brown arm.

Thank heaven for Malcolm, Liz mused thankfully as she went to the shed and began to sort out riding caps and print names on slips of white paper. By now he understood the intricacies of the special safety gear and knew exactly what had to be done.

Even Evelyn and Stan appeared to be affected by the general air of excitement this morning. When the first ambulance nosed its way in the entrance, Evelyn called to Liz, busy in the paddock below. But Liz too had caught sight of the vehicles and already she was hurrying back up the path. Presently private cars and a second ambulance were grouped on the grass and Liz found herself the centre of a cluster of doctors, therapists and ambulance drivers.

With swift efficiency wheelchairs were lifted down from vehicles and boys and girls were carried from cars, some to mount their crutches, others, unable to stand, slithered along the grass with the peculiar, fish-like motion with which Liz was so familiar from her period of nursing such patients. But there was no doubt as to the happiness of the atmosphere. Laughing, excited children's faces, the cheerful ambulance drivers, all out in the clear sunshiny air. It'll work, Liz told herself, I know it will! Aloud she set out to explain to the doctors the quiet temperament of the ponies she had chosen for the special riders, the neck-straps and safety stirrups, the webbing belts with their sturdy handles at the back of the rider. 'So you see,' she finished, 'I don't see how anything can go wrong.'

'Nor me.' The leader of the medical team, a slightly elderly man with an international reputation for his success in the field of children's diseases, sent her an appreciative glance. 'I can't see anything but good coming of it, Miss Kennedy,' he told her in his quiet tones. 'A great scheme. Why not give each child a ride on the ponies?' He was counting heads. 'You have sufficient mounts?'

Liz nodded eagerly. 'I can take them all for a ride today, that is, if you can spare the time to wait? It would be a pity if anyone had to miss out. From your point of view as well as theirs,' she explained in her soft husky tones.

'That's what I'm here for!' An expression of interest and approval lighted the wise, lined face. 'Let's give them all a try-out and see, shall we? We'll soon pick out which ones could benefit by the exercise.'

All at once everyone was busily engaged in pushing wheelchairs towards the ramp, arranging which children would be in the first section to try out the new venture. Malcolm stood alongside the tea-tree railing, ready to free the ponies when the small riders were mounted.

'Miss Kennedy! Miss Kennedy!' The radiant face of a small fair-haired girl was turned towards Liz. 'It's Julie!' The childish tones rang with sheer happiness. 'You're *here*! You went away and I thought I was never going to see you again, ever, ever, ever! Miss Kennedy, am I going to ride? *Really* ride?'

'You are, darling!' Liz dropped a kiss on the blonde curls, gave the child a warm hug. 'Look, Julie, I've got a little pony specially for you! He's called Pinocchio. Remember how you used to ask me to read you the story?'

'Pinocchio! I'm going to ride Pinocchio!' Blue eyes sparkled with excitement as she swung around. 'Daddy! This is the nurse I told you about—the one I like!'

For the first time Liz became aware of a man standing behind the child's wheelchair. Slim and small-boned, wearing dark sun-glasses, immaculately dressed in a light-weight summer suit, he appeared to be in his early forties. 'So you're Julie's father?' Liz smiled across at him. 'At the hospital Julie was always telling me about you too!'

He laughed and said in cultured tones, 'It's a splendid job you're doing here with these kids, Miss Kennedy!'

'Oh, I get a lot of fun out of it!' She was adjusting a riding cap over the silky fair curls. Then, pinning a slip of paper with JULIE written in large letters to the small girl's blouse, she turned to him. 'If you'll give me a hand, Mr. Ridgway, we'll lift Julie up on to the saddle.' The mount was one of the ponies she had purchased at the recent sale and Liz was pleased to find that the black pony stood perfectly still as the small burden was settled on the broad back.

With deft movements the man slipped the child's helpless feet into stirrup cups while Liz adjusted the length of the leathers. She threw the reins over the pony's sturdy head and Julie, laughing, wild with excitement, clasped the reins in small hands. Liz passed the halter rope to the man standing beside her. 'If you'll just hold Pinocchio while I go and see how the others are getting along?'

'He doesn't look to me as though he's got any ideas of making a run for it. Looks more as though he's thinking of taking a morning siesta.'

'I know,' Liz laughed lightly. 'That's how we like them!' She moved on towards the next pony waiting at the railing.

'Danny!' A loose-limbed boy, tall for his fourteen years, glanced up from his wheelchair and smiled nervously. Pale eyes in a thin unchildlike face slid towards the overweight Palomino. 'Miss Kennedy,' only too well she recognized the hesitant speech, the apprehensive note in the weak tones, 'he ... looks so big ... doesn't he?'

'He only seems like that from down here,' she said gently. 'Once you're up on his back you'll feel differently about him. Just think, Danny, up there you'll be higher than I am, higher than anyone on the ground!'

'Will I?' He swallowed nervously and Liz saw the fear glimmering in his eyes.

'Come along, Danny.' The physiotherapist, a cheerful motherly-looking woman whom Liz remembered from her work at the Institute, came to stand beside the boy's wheelchair. She slipped a riding cap on his head and adjusted the strap beneath his chin. 'You're next!'

'No.' He drew back, nervous and afraid. 'I can't! I can't!' he whispered piteously.

'We'll help you,' Liz told him reassuringly. 'There'll be someone at each side of the pony to hold you on every minute. You couldn't fall off, even if you wanted to, and I'll lead the pony along. Just a little way, no further than the gate, unless you want to go on. You might, you know. Well, Danny, what do you say?'

'I ... I ... want to ... but I can't——'

'Just this once—for me?' Liz pleaded in her soft husky tones.

'All right, then, I'll ... try.' Terror shone in the pale eyes as with infinite gentleness Liz, assisted by an ambulance driver and a woman therapist, lifted the trembling lad from the wheelchair and threw the hanging legs over the saddle.

Clutching the reins in a convulsive grip, Danny sat rigid with fear. Liz reached up to lay an encouraging hand on his thin arm. 'It's not so bad, is it? My goodness, you are high up!' After a few moments she felt a slight relaxation in the tense muscles. A nervous smile flickered across the pale face.

'You'll stay with me, Miss Kennedy, won't you?'

'Every single minute. That's a promise!'

A swift glance around her assured her that there were ample helpers, doctors, therapists, ambulance men, to lift the remaining children up on to their mounts. So she remained at the boy's side. She didn't want to risk losing her small victory, for it was a victory! Danny, who appeared to be so tall, so nearly grown up, and yet at heart was such a helpless small boy, afraid of attempting anything new, afraid of almost everything! Liz had never become reconciled to the sight of the weak, loose-limbed figure slithering along the floor of the Institute. Perhaps she felt specially concerned for him because she was aware of the doctors' verdict that it was the boy's nervousness that prevented him from making any progress in his condition. His fears stood in the way of his making any effort to be taught to walk on crutches or to help himself in any way. Danny, she knew, was one of the chief factors in her determination to start a riding school for such children. If only she could succeed in gaining his confidence, just get him to sit on a pony, he would have taken a terrific step forward. Before long he might even gain sufficient confidence to learn to use crutches, maybe progress sufficiently to try and make himself walk, even if it were in an odd awkward manner. It was a special dream she had cherished for a long time. Now the sight of Danny fighting his terror and actually seated on his mount brought an unexpected moisture to her eyes.

'Look at me! I'm a cowboy! Gettyup there!' A small Maori boy gave his mount a resounding slap. Fortunately the somnolent pony was too lazy to respond to the gesture. Somehow Liz couldn't find it in her heart to reprimand Taiere, not today when he was finding a new mobility, even if only temporarily. White teeth gleamed in a wide and happy grin. 'What's his name, Miss Kennedy?' Before she could think of a suitable reply, for the pony was one she had purchased recently at the sale and was as yet unnamed, the high childish treble ran on, 'Betcha he's got a real cowboy name! A neat horse like him! Betcha he could go real fast, catch Injuns and everything! I gotta call him *something*!'

Hurriedly Liz searched her mind for a dashing name for the plump pony, now blinking sleepily in the hot sunshine.

'Pancho!' she cried at last.

Taiere's broad grin widened. 'I *knew* he was a real cowboy horse!' The bloodcurdling yell he let out might have been that of one of his ancestors, a century earlier, as he rushed into battle with an enemy tribe. 'Yahoo! I'm a cowboy! Look out, you kids, here I come!'

He was utterly content and Liz knew that while he waited astride a rough ungainly little pony, all the time Taiere was in another, more exciting world, speeding over the sagebrush, rounding up a bunch of broncos, galloping at high speed after a steer, lassoo in hand.

Her glance moved down the lines of mounts to where a girl, taller and older than the rest, was being lifted from her wheelchair. Showing a slight nervousness but happy and excited too, Gillian allowed herself to be put astride Red's back. Good old Red, I knew he wouldn't let me down, Liz thought. How patiently he was standing, almost as though he understood what was required of him with this new type of rider. Liz watched as the helpless girl was settled in the saddle, the reins placed in nervous hands,

Before long helpful kindly hands had lifted the first lot of children up on their mounts. On this first occasion Liz planned that there would be no lessons given. Later on when the riders had learned to feel the movement, they would be taught how to make the pony stop and go, even to rise to a trot, but today was a matter for the medical experts to decide which children would benefit most from the exercise.

When all the riders had had a chance to accustom themselves to their new unaccustomed position they set off. Liz was a little apprehensive about Danny.

Would he lose his newly-gained confidence and once again fall a victim to his fears, once he felt himself in motion? She kept a firm hold on the safety belt as they moved away from the ramp, but although rigid with anxiety he made no protest. Perhaps she thought he was endeavouring to hide his terror from his small companions.

The medical men joined the party of riders and helpers and it was a happy group who set off across the dried grass of the paddock. Glancing back over her shoulder, Liz waved to Evelyn and Stan, watching from the yard. Nearby the children awaiting their turn to ride looked happily occupied as they played with kittens, dog and bantams. Liz was glad now that she had had the forethought to provide something the children could amuse themselves with while they were awaiting their turn to try out their new mobility.

'We're away!' Julie's father was smiling towards her. 'My rider's in a sort of seventh heaven of delight. How's yours?'

'He's coming along, aren't you, Danny?'

The boy nodded, obviously too strung-up and tense to make a reply.

One of the medical team, a serious-eyed young man with a pleasant smile, came to join Liz. 'Don't you believe it! Danny's doing fine!' He dropped his voice to a lower note. 'I'll tell you something, Miss Kennedy. I've got great hopes for this venture of yours.'

'Thank you.' Liz guided the pony away from the spreading branches of a peach tree high overhead.

He strolled along at her side over the grass.

'If you get this one used to the motion, get the better of that fear-complex of his, then I'd say the battle was half won. Could be he'd be inspired to take another step, and another. It would spur him on to greater efforts in other directions——'

Liz threw him a brief sideways glance. 'You mean,' she whispered, 'he might have a go at crutches?'

'That's what I'm getting at. Who knows? Later on he might even have a crack at getting himself mobile.'

'That's what I'm hoping too. Do you think there's a

chance?'

'After this,' the doctor jerked his head towards the silent rider, gave a significant smile, 'I'll believe anything can happen! You're doing a fine job, Miss Kennedy! Keep it up!'

Liz didn't quite know what to say. 'I haven't proved a thing yet. But I will! I know I will!'

'You're working along the right lines. You know,' they were matching their gait to the ponies' short jerky steps, 'as far as I can tell there isn't one of these disabled kids who wouldn't benefit from this open air and exercise, maybe far more than we can imagine, so long as the lessons are held under medical supervision, of course. Funny thing,' he was speaking as if to himself, 'how riding seems to relax the muscles of these cases of spastic deplegia and typical scissor gait. Yet the same muscles react violently to any other sort of effort to make them respond.'

'That's what I thought too,' Liz said eagerly. 'Oh, I know of course that they'll all benefit from the exercise, but I'm counting on something else as well——'

'I know what you're getting at! The psychological angle, the feeling of achievement that riding gives these crippled kids, from a therapeutic angle, I mean, not just for pleasure. You know as well as I do I expect, that one of the problems we have in the school for these cases is exercising in trying to get their legs apart. Sitting on a horse, they do it automatically.' His voice was thoughtful as he gazed around the happy faces. 'A new dimension for them and boy, do they need one!'

Liz nodded. 'Far enough, do you think?'

'I would say so, for the first time!'

Liz turned the pony's head and the procession moved back over the grassy paddock. She realised that Danny's tenseness had lessened, though he still held a convulsive grip on the reins. Not like Taiere, who was calling and laughing, urging his pony on with wild calls, his small dark face still split in a huge happy grin.

When they got back to the ramp once again the

ponies stood quietly, patiently waiting while the riders were lifted carefully down from the saddles and re-seated in wheelchairs. Presently the other group of children took their turn in being settled on the ponies. It was difficult to determine, Liz mused, which were the happier or more excited, the section who had al-ready had their ride or the group now starting on their new mobility.

This time Liz helped Sandra up on to a pony. A pretty girl of twelve years, she was lovely to look at, cheerful and smiling, normal in every way—except one! Lewis Ridgway steadied the girl from the oppo-site side and Liz found herself thinking that he was the type of man who would always be found where he could be of help, quietly, efficiently there! How alike they were, he and Julie. The man with his dark clever face and the bright child with her impish smile and alart mind. A tragedy for a parent—and yet who could feel sadness for a child who was so transparently happy, especially today! She glanced back to where Julie, cuddling a kitten on her lap, chatted brightly from her wheelchair.

There was an atmosphere of happiness and excite-ment in the barn as the children returned and with appetites sharpened by unaccustomed outdoor exer-cise, began to open their packed lunches they had brought with them.

Malcolm volunteered to make coffee for the guests while Stan wielded a massive enamel teapot and liz poured orange cordial into glasses and passed them along the table. A moment later Evelyn entered the barn bearing a huge platter of steaming hot scones.

A little later Liz's small figure was almost concealed by the group of medical men and physiotherapists sur-rounding her, all talking eagerly. There was no doubt but that the experiment had proved a success and given a chance, promised to be all she hoped it would be. At last she managed to put the query that was uppermost in her mind. 'I was wondering,' she turned towards a doctor standing at her side, an elderly man with a kindly face and a slow deliberate manner of speech, 'how many of the children would benefit by the exercise?'

He balanced his beaker of coffee thoughtfully, a twinkle in the grey eyes. 'My dear girl, the whole damn lot, and I'm confident I'm speaking for everyone here when I say it!'

'Of course!' There was a chorus of agreement. 'No question about that!'

'Take young Danny,' a younger doctor put in. 'All that's holding him back from making any progress at all is sheer nervousness. But give him a few lessons here——' He turned enquiringly towards Liz. 'How many did you intend giving to make up the course?'

'Ten,' she answered promptly, adding after a moment, 'but of course if anyone wanted to keep on after that they'll be welcome to do so.'

All at once everyone was talking at once, but the discussion was short and unanimous. The medical experts agreed that providing the school was run under medical supervision with therapists in attendance at all times, every child there would benefit. That apart from the therapeutic value of the riding in strengthening muscle and helping co-ordination, the psychological benefit to the children would be considerable.

The picnic meal was almost over when Liz caught the sound of feminine voices outside the barn. Threading her way through groups of wheelchairs, she made her way to the doorway. Two women stood framed in the opening and Liz found herself meeting icy blue eyes. Beryl!' What had brought her here? Curiosity perhaps to find out how the new girl was getting along with her crazy scheme? Or was she being uncharitable, for the other girl was smiling. 'Oh, Miss Kennedy, I do hope we're not interrupting anything? This is my aunt Olga.' The tall slight woman with silvery hair gave a gentle smile. 'We wondered if you were hiring out horses to ordinary riders. Actually it's for my son Darryl that I'm enquiring.'

'Of course you're not interrupting anything. Come inside.' Liz led the way into the barn. The two women followed her and at the long table where doctors and therapists were grouped, Liz made the introductions. 'Coffee?' she enquired. 'Malcolm will bring you a fresh cup.'

'Coffee coming up!' Already he was moving towards the bubbling percolator on an electric hotplate.

'How old is Darryl?' Liz enquired politely.

'Oh, he's thirteen,' Beryl answered. 'I thought it would be a splendid chance for him to learn to ride while we're staying in the country.'

'But,' Liz's mind went to the large sheep station over the hills, 'haven't you any horses on your own property?'

'Haven't had for years. Sandy's in charge there now, but he prefers to use a tractor and Land-Rover so ... Thing is, Darryl thinks he can ride, but actually he's never been up on a horse in his life.'

'We couldn't risk anything happening to him,' the slim grey-haired woman put in in her hesitant tones. 'That's why Beryl wants a proper riding school where he could be taught. You know how it is ... an only child ...'

'Well, nothing's going to happen to him here,' her niece cut in impatiently, 'not with the old nags Miss Kennedy's got around the place! And don't forget that she's trained to look after kids. It's her job.'

She made it sound, Liz thought with tightened lips, as though children were some sort of household pets. 'Actually,' Liz said, 'I don't hire out horses. Maybe you could find someone in the district who does?'

'Not a chance.' Beryl shrugged, her attitude giving the impression that one stupid woman running a riding school in the district was quite sufficient, thank you.

'Please take him, Miss Kennedy,' pleaded the older woman. 'If you only knew how much he's set his heart on it.'

Liz couldn't help thinking that young Darryl Manning had all the indications of being a rebellious and indulged youngster. But the timid older woman seemed genuinely friendly, even if somewhat under the dominance of her stronger-minded niece. Chances were, she told herself hopefully, that the boy would soon tire of his new activity held under supervision.

'All right, then.' She was aware of the doctors waiting to make their farewells. 'Shall we say Wednesday afternoon? If you'll excuse me ... it looks as though the drivers are in a hurry to get back to town.'

Liz moved towards Julie and began to guide the wheelchair towards the opening. 'Did you enjoy it?'

'Oh, it was super! Miss Kennedy, can I come every week? My pony, he'll know me again when he sees me, won't he?'

'Of course, darling.'

'I know why he's called Pinocchio. It's because he's so little. That's right, isn't it, Daddy?'

Liz became aware of the slight dark-haired man who had come to join them. 'Here, let me do that——' He took hold of the wheelchair and for a second his hand rested on Liz's fingers. She drew back with a laugh. 'If you insist!' She blinked, all at once aware of the depth of feeling in Lewis Ridgway's glance.

'I'll be in the first lot to have a turn at riding next time, won't I, Miss Kennedy?' The child's face was radiant with happiness.

'I'll have Pinocchio all ready for you,' Liz promised. 'He'll be tied up and waiting at the rail.'

Out in the yard Julie was carried by her father into the waiting car. He said goodbye to Liz, then paused, a hand resting on the starter. 'Don't forget, if you need any more helpers out here on riding days, I'm always available. Call on me any time at all!'

'Do I need helpers?' she laughed lightly. 'I want all I can get! I'm planning to put some articles about the riding centre in the city papers, get a feature included in the news section on television too if I can. I thought it might all help to attract some publicity, get me some new helpers so we can run on a sort of roster system. Of course I wouldn't say "no" if someone offers a nice fat donation to the fund! If you could fit it in to come out with Julie each week it would be wonderful, but ...' She hesitated. Hadn't she once heard that Lewis Ridgway held an important position in the city?

'That is, if you can spare the time?'

'Nothing else is important enough to stop me from coming out here.' His voice held an oddly significant note.

Julie waved back to Liz as the opulent-looking car joined the line of vehicles moving up the driveway. When Liz turned back she was surprised to find Beryl at her side, and something in the other girl's speculative glance made Liz rush wildly into speech. 'His wife died some years ago—that's why Julie lives at the Crippled Children's Institute. I guess he'd do just about anything for her, even if it means coming away out here to the riding centre each week.'

'Just for Julie?'

Liz was annoyed to feel the pink creeping up her cheeks, then she was even more annoyed to notice the light shrug of the other girl's shoulders, the mocking lift of her lips. If it wasn't so utterly absurd she would argue the matter, but that would serve merely to lend the ridiculous assumption an air of truth. As if Julie's father had the slightest feeling for her personally.

She couldn't understand the other girl's ill-will. Jealousy? But that too was surely beyond the bounds of possibility, for how could anyone so wildly beautiful grudge another girl so trifling a thing as a stranger's glance of approval? Could it be her harmless friendship with Peter Farraday that sparked off Beryl's deliberate hostility? *Who's jealous now?* Liz wrenched the random thoughts aside and turned to make her farewells to the waiting group of doctors.

'Goodbye! Goodbye! See you next week!' In a matter of minutes the ambulance drivers had loaded their vehicles with passengers and wheelchairs, and were driving away. They were followed by Beryl and her aunt, the gleaming car glinting in the afternoon sunshine.

As she strolled back to the barn Liz puzzled once again as to the reason why Beryl's flawless features seemed so hauntingly familiar. She couldn't possibly have met her before, and yet . . .

The barn when she reached it seemed curiously

empty and silent, with only Evelyn moving around the tables collecting ashtrays and Stan wielding a massive broom as he swept up crumbs and lunch papers. Liz was stacking cups and beakers on a wicker tray when Malcolm thrust his head in at the doorway. 'I've brushed down the ponies, put them all back in the paddocks. Pretty lucky bunch, that lot! A few strolls up the paddock and they're off duty for a week. How about if I put a couple of them in the corral for to-night? Might get a bit of weight off them.'

Liz nodded. 'That's an idea! I was getting around to suggesting you do that——'

'Oh, I've got lots of ideas! Here's another. I've got a spare radiogram kicking around the place at home. We could shove it into the barn here——'

Liz said, 'That would be marvellous for the children. I could get some special records——'

'I wasn't,' Malcolm said with a grin, 'thinking of the children, but I'll bring it down just the same.'

'Thank you.'

'My pleasure. It's all for the cause—— Look, Liz, they're putting on a dance down in the local hall to-night. Funds are in aid of young Riki Manu, and just about everyone in the place is going along.'

'Not the young Maori boy who's making such a name for himself with his singing?'

'That's him! He comes from around this district and the locals are raising funds to help get him started on a career overseas. But it's not just to give Riki a helping hand that I'd like to go. If I could take you along ... what do you say? I mean,' he was suddenly overcome with embarrassment, 'if you're not doing anything special——'

'Love to go!' She felt so elated she was in the mood for celebrating, and it was a long time since she'd attended a country 'do', with its warmth and family atmosphere and informality.

'I know I'll be sorry about this,' Malcolm muttered morosely. 'It's always the same at these country hops, swags more guys than girls. I won't even get a look in!'

'Don't worry,' Liz was gathering crockery and stacking it in piles on the tray, 'I'll save you the first dance.'

'That's more like it! See you tonight, then.' She was scarcely aware he had gone, she was so delighted with the way in which things had turned out. It would have spoiled her satisfaction in the day had any of the children been forced to miss out in the matter of future rides, but now each one was included in the project. It was all working out just as she'd dreamed. Lots of difficulties ahead, of course, but she felt confident now of coping with them. Malcolm's invitation to the local gathering had set the seal on the day's sense of achievement, and with or without music Liz could have danced around the barn in sheer joy. Everyone would be at the hall tonight, Malcolm had said, so surely Peter ... she couldn't *wait* to let him know of their success!

CHAPTER 5

WHEN Malcolm arrived to escort Liz to the dance being held that evening in the local hall, a cool breeze was stirring the grass of the paddocks and the pines on the hilltop were a serrated black outline against the lemon afterglow of sunset.

She closed the door of the darkened cottage behind her and ran down the steps, aware all the time that Malcolm seemed to have difficulty in wrenching his gaze away.

'Gee, Liz, I hardly knew you!' She had drawn the long hair high in a topknot, revealing a piquant profile, the big eyes were accented with turquoise shadow and the long skirt swirling around her ankles lent her small figure a youthful and appealing dignity.

She laughed mockingly as they went down the path together. 'It's me all right!' Nevertheless she felt a moment's pleasure in the sincerity of the compliment, even if it came only from young Malcolm who in this isolated area would scarcely meet a new girl from one month to the next. She was glad now that at the last minute before leaving town she had crammed into her bulging travel bag a filmy long-sleeved blouse, caught at the wrists, together with the flowing skirt with its gay patchwork of colours.

'I never knew you could look like that!' The boyish gaze still lingered on Liz as they paused beside the scarlet sports car.

'That,' said Liz, seating herself in the passenger seat, 'is because you're so used to seeing me in ancient jodhpurs, with the odd streak of mud on my face, smelling of horse. You know?'

'Not tonight! And that's not what I meant.' He sniffed appreciatively. 'What is it, Liz, that perfume you're using?'

'White ginger, and it's the real thing. A girl-friend brought it back for me from a holiday in Hawaii. Like it?'

'Do I? How you expect me to keep my mind on driving——' He thumbed the starter and they shot backwards up the drive. Tyres scrunched on loose metal as the car swung around in the roadway, then they went hurtling down the shadowed path in a direction that was new to Liz. Stones rattled against the undercarriage of the vehicle and dark bush flashed past on either side. Presently they shot up a straight stretch of the highway, screamed around a fern-concealed bend and came in sight of a long timber building where light streamed out through doors open to the summer night. Swinging in at the entrance, they bumped over the rough ground to merge into a cluster of cars, trucks and Land-Rovers parked on the grassy space.

As they strolled towards the hall strains of music drifted towards them. Once inside it seemed to Liz, pushing her way through groups milling around the doorway, that everyone living within miles of the hall must have converged here tonight. Seated on long forms set around the edge of the dance floor were girls in vividly patterned frocks, men wearing shirts, shorts, sandals. There was a sprinkling of older folk, middle-aged farmers and their wives, and children skated excitedly at the fringe of the polished floorboards. For Liz progress was slow, for Malcolm apparently knew everyone here. On all sides he was greeted by calls and teasing remarks. To her, however, the only familiar faces were those of Stan and Evelyn. They had left the house before her and were now waving and smiling towards her from the opposite side of the hall. At that moment she caught sight of Tim and Wayne, and her heart gave an unexpected lurch. If the two station hands from Arundel were here tonight then perhaps Peter too ... Her swift glance raked the crowd, but obviously he wasn't here.

Presently the insistent beat of pop music surged around them and she and Malcolm moved into the crowd milling around the glassy floor. High above, coloured streamers and balloons hung from the rafters and electric lamp bulbs sheathed in pink crêpe paper shed their soft glow over the shifting scene.

From the moment when Liz first set foot on the floor she found herself sought after by various partners, dancing, dancing to the tempo provided by three Maori youths who played a banjo, piano and guitar. All the time she moved to the foot-tapping rhythm she found herself stealing glances towards the entrance doors, wondering if Peter would put in an appearance. Not that she cared, one way or the other. It was all the same to her. Even if he did come here he would be with Beryl. Not that she minded about that either! All she was concerned about was a little matter of letting him know that in spite of his initial lack of encouragement she had proved herself capable of carrying out a task that she suspected he considered beyond her powers. As the evening wore on, however, she ceased to glance towards the open doorway. She might as well face the fact that he wasn't coming. A pity, for what satisfaction in a victory where one's opponent wasn't even aware of his defeat? In a pause between dances she realised the evening's compère was making an announcement from the stage. 'Will you take your partners for the supper waltz, please?'

The Maori group of musicians swung into the familiar, heart-catching rhythm of *Some Day, My Love*, and Tim, who had partnered her through the last intoxicating pop tune, hesitated, wiping his hot face with a handkerchief. 'Sorry,' he murmured uncomfortably, 'but I'm not too good at waltzing. Never got the hang of it somehow. How about you?'

They were standing together on the fringe of the dance floor. 'I learned ballroom when——' She never finished the sentence, for glancing up at that moment she found Peter at her side, tall and bronzed and vibrantly good-looking. All at once the evening seemed to come alive. Meeting his grin, she was filled with an electric excitement.

'Shall we?' Without giving her time to reply he

swept her away. Liz's patchwork skirt whirled around her ankles in a swirling kaleidoscope of colour as they swept the length of the hall, watched by the onlookers seated and standing at the edge of the floor. Liz took pride in her ballroom dancing, although she had had few opportunities to practise it, but never had she had a partner such as this. It was as if they were moulded together, steps and rhythm merging perfectly. She was unaware of the ring of watchers, the sudden hush that had fallen over the crowded gathering. Even when applause rang around them it scarcely touched her. Presently other couples rose to join what had become an exhibition dance. Confetti showered around them, paper streamers flew through the air and twirled among the dancers. Someone cut the strings of clustered balloons and the coloured shapes drifted down from the rafters high above to mingle with the blue smoke of the hall. Still Liz and Peter danced on in silence.

At length the music drew to a close and for a moment they stood motionless. He drew a long pink paper streamer from her topknot and Liz raised a flushed face to meet his enigmatical smile. 'You're almost one of us already, Liz!'

'Yes, aren't I? Malcolm brought me along—it seems ages ago now. I thought you were never coming!'

The moment the words were out she would have given anything to recall them. No use hoping he would let her off, pretend he hadn't noticed that last betraying phrase. He didn't.

'So you missed me?' He was laughing at her.

'No, no, of course not! It was just,' she floundered unhappily on, 'that Malcolm said everyone would be here tonight and I——' She was saved by the group on the stage as once again they broke into a waltz rhythm and in the joy of movement with this man who was the partner every girl dreamed of, everything else, even her hopelessly incurable habit of blurting out whatever happened to enter her mind at that particular moment, was forgotten.

As the waltz came to an end, masculine hands carried from a back room of the hall long trestle tables heaped with a profusion of home-baked cakes, lavishly spread with fresh cream, sandwiches and seafood savouries. The last notes faded into silence and Peter guided her towards the tables, then left her to join a group at the opposite end of the hall. Oh, she might have known—she had known all along, only she wouldn't allow herself to admit it—that he wouldn't come here alone. Why then should she feel this sickening sense of let-down at the sight of Beryl? Tonight the older girl appeared more attention-worthy than ever in a deceptively simple black frock, setting off to advantage her silver-gilt hair and fair skin. Just as Peter, tall and dark and distinguished, provided a perfect foil for Beryl's blonde beauty. She wouldn't allow herself to think of either of them! Determinedly she flashed a smile towards Malcolm, who at the moment was plying her with an outsized sausage roll and a thick china cup of steaming tea. Thank heaven for Malcolm, young and naïve, anxious only to serve her. He would never know how much he was helping her in merely being here with her tonight, bless him. Almost without her own volition her gaze strayed back to the knot of people standing opposite. Beryl was chatting vivaciously with Sandy on one side of her and Peter on the other. At that moment, catching Liz's glance, she sent her a nod of a pale-gold head, a gesture clearly meant to indicate that Liz was worth no more than a careless nod of recognition. Beryl's aunt Olga flashed Liz a warm and friendly smile, then Liz's glance moved to the boy standing at the edge of the group. He appeared to be small for his age, with lanky fair hair and a sulky expression. She couldn't help thinking that Darryl, in his high-fashion jacket and tailored slacks, appeared oddly out of place among the casually attired boys of his own age who were here tonight.

When supper was over the compère mounted the stage and gave a short address on the object of the night's entertainment, the proceeds of which were to go towards financing the study of the popular young entertainer and composer, their own local boy, Riki Manu. 'And just to let you know how much he appreciates what you people of his home town are doing for him, he's made a special trip up from the South Island to be with us tonight. I give you—Riki Manu, who's going to favour us with one of his own compositions!'

The compère's voice was drowned in a thunder of applause as a smiling young Maori youth took the stage. Well-built, beautifully spoken, with all the relaxed charm and ease of manner of his race, he plucked at the guitar slung over his shoulder. The notes fell into a pool of silence, then the singer's voice with its rich cadence took up the melody.

A deafening clapping echoed through the building as the song came to an end. Again and again the young entertainer was recalled by the crowd to sing still more of his compositions, until at last he bowed himself off the stage and the group moved back to their instruments.

Trestle tables were carried away to the rear of the hall and once again the beat of a popular hit tune pulsated through the smoke-filled air. Liz was aware of Peter standing with a group of young farmers, apparently deep in conversation. Out of the corner of her eye she noticed Beryl, her laughing face upturned towards Sandy as he guided her towards the dance floor. Liz waited ... and waited ... making various excuses to hopeful partners as the minutes ticked away. Would he, or wouldn't he, approach her once again? All at once she realised that far from acquainting him with the news of her success, so far she had barely spoken two words to him, and what she had said had been quite disastrous. Would fate send her a second chance in order to even the score?

It seemed, however, that she had lost her opportunity, at least so far as tonight was concerned, for as dance followed dance and Liz was eagerly sought after by various partners, Peter did not again seek her out. Maybe he wasn't interested in ballroom dancing. But the next minute as she moved to the beat of the latest hit tune, she caught sight of him and Beryl taking the floor. For a few seconds they were obscured from her view, then through a gap on the crowded floor she glimpsed them once again. How relaxed and carefree they appeared, like old friends ... *or lovers reunited*. Beryl was chatting with gay animation. She wouldn't ever say the wrong thing at the worst possible time! And he? Unconsciously she sighed. With Peter you never could tell, but he looked happy enough, no doubt about that.

For the remainder of the evening it seemed to Liz that Beryl was on the dance floor as continuously as she herself, sharing her dances between Peter and her manager. Liz found herself wondering what it would feel like to find oneself as confident, as lovely and sought-after as the other girl. To have two men competing anxiously for her favours. Not that Liz had any lack of partners. Inevitably she was on the dance floor from the moment the Maori group of musicians struck up the first notes of the pop music, but it wasn't quite the same thing.

It was long after midnight when the final dance of the evening was announced. When Malcolm approached her she went with him towards the dance floor without a backward glance. Not that she need have concerned herself, she told herself a little later, for Peter was nowhere to be seen. She was surprised therefore when the dance ended to realise he was striding purposefully towards them and even more astonished to realise it was Malcolm whom he was seeking out.

'I've got a message to pass on to you, mate,' he told the younger man. 'Happened to be outside just now having a smoke and old Toby went past in his car. Stopped for a minute to tell me that he was in the devil of a hurry to push on, his wife's not well and he had to get back as soon as he could. Said to get the word to you that your brother David's struck trouble on the road a few miles back. No danger ... he's run into a ditch and wants you to come and pull him back on the road, give him a hand to get mobile again.'

Malcolm's young face fell. 'He *would* choose tonight

95

to get himself in the ditch! He's a rotten driver—I'm always telling him. I've half a mind to leave him there to sweat it out till morning. Teach him a lesson!' He gave a rueful grin, said on a note of resignation, 'But I guess I'll have to go into the big rescue act. Where exactly is he?'

'On the side road just opposite Maybury's farm! Get it?'

'I wish I didn't! I'll kill that brother of mine one of these days!' He drew a palm across his throat in a sinister gesture, then turned to Liz, a note of regret in his voice. 'I'm sorry about this. You do understand——'

'Don't worry,' Peter's even tones gave nothing away, 'I'll see Liz back to the cottage.'

'That's okay, then.'

'Thanks for bringing me tonight,' she smiled appealingly up at the downcast boyish face.

'Pleasure. Well, see you.' He threw a rueful grin over his shoulder, then turned reluctantly away. A moment later he was lost among the crowd surging towards the open doorway.

No one, thought Liz, had taken the trouble to enquire of her if she minded being taken care of like a parcel by Peter and faithfully delivered back to her destination. She wasn't sure that she wanted to be escorted back there by him. There was something about him, something male and masterful and definitely disturbing. She had a suspicion, that alone with him in the darkness and intimacy of the car, it might be difficult to make herself remember that he belonged to someone else—well, near enough to make no difference! All at once she wanted to escape the drive home with Peter. Peter, who had danced practically all evening with Beryl. Wildly she said: 'It's okay, I can go home with Stan and Evelyn.'

'You can't, you know, they've just left!'

'We could catch them up.'

'No.' He shook a dark head.

'Why not?'

'Just that I prefer it this way.'

'Oh!' Liz thought over what he had said. She didn't

quite know what to make of it. Besides, there was something in his voice that was affecting her oddly. He couldn't mean, he must mean ... She hesitated, then made one last effort. 'But what about ... Beryl?'

It wasn't her night, she told herself the next moment, for saying the right thing, for he was regarding her with a hard stare. 'Beryl?'

As if he didn't know what she meant! 'I thought,' she faltered in the face of his cool enquiring look, 'that you'd come with a party tonight. You know, Beryl, her aunt, Sandy McPhail——'

'That's right.' Ice tinkled in his tones.

'I wouldn't want to put you to any trouble——'

'No trouble.' Coolly he took her arm. 'Let's get out of this mob, shall we?' He was guiding her through the throng and out into the clear night air where the stars of the Southern Cross hung like spangles against a backdrop of pulsing purple-blue.

In silence he guided the car out of the cluster of moving vehicles that were bumping along the rutted ground, then they swung into the tree-shadowed road, and still Liz could find nothing to say. There was a compelling attraction about the dark profile outlined in the dim light of the dashboard. She couldn't seem to wrench her gaze away.

Around them the bush-clad hills rose dark and mysterious, smudged shapes against the clear night sky. A native owl flew past the windscreen and was lost in the darkness and on an empty stretch ahead, a 'possum, dazzled by the gleam of headlamps, crouched motionless in the roadway, then within a second of death, the furry creature scampered away among the dust-coated ferns at the side of the highway.

'How'd you make out today?'

With an effort she brought her mind back to the matter in hand. This was the question she'd waited for, she reminded herself. Maybe if she didn't look at him it might be easier to think of ... important things ... like the answers she had rehearsed in her mind to tell him.

'Today?' She was well aware he was referring to the

start of her venture, but she was determined to take her time, make the most of her victory. 'You mean——'

'You know what I mean, Liz.' He threw her a smiling glance and suddenly she felt her spirits soar into such a state of high excitement that all the cool confident phrases she had so carefully practised fled from her mind. Instead she heard herself say warmly: 'Oh, it was fabulous! A real success! Each one of the children had a ride, so that the medical men could form an opinion as to whether it would really help them, and what do you know? I've got the green light to go right ahead with the riding school! I'm going to make it a course of ten lessons,' she ran on excitedly, 'then if they're getting real benefit from the riding, and I know they will, they can keep on coming out each week if they want to. The doctors and therapists were awfully enthusiastic about the idea!'

'Good for you!' His eyes were on a fern-concealed bend in the darkness ahead. 'How many kids turned up in the end?'

'Everyone came, just as I was hoping! Twenty-seven altogether, and each one of the children is to keep on with the course. I was so glad that no one was left out.'

'And you're planning on helping the whole bunch of them?'

Once again the special smile he seemed to keep for Liz Kennedy and her idiosyncrasies was having an effect on her, piercing her defences. She was having trouble in keeping her mind on her venture, or on anything else, for that matter. She wished she could keep on looking at him for ever.

'Twenty-seven miracles! Isn't that rather a tall order, even for you?'

'I ... wouldn't say so.' Something in the atmosphere, maybe the deep softening of his tone, was doing things to her, making it awfully difficult to think of anything else, even the children.

'You sure must believe in miracles, Liz!'

'Oh, I do! I do!'

'Make them happen, hmm?'

'If I can,' she said faintly. A crazy, impossible longing was tumbling wildly through her brain. If only she could order one more miracle, the biggest, most important one of all ... that he should fall in love with her instead of Beryl.

'So now,' with an effort she brought her mind back to his voice, 'with the place more or less in order——'

She pulled her thoughts back to some sort of order, said quickly: 'And with the ponies you helped me to get at the sale, I can go right ahead. The big fat cheque I got in the mail from nice Mr. X made all the difference——'

'Mr. X, the unknown?'

'That's him. Only I always think of him as Mr. Executive. I've got this mental picture of him——'

'Such as?'

All at once it was easy to confide her hopes and dreams to Peter, even to let him in on her silly imaginings regarding her unknown donor. 'I've got him all figured out. City guy, not too young. He's big and stout and just a bit pompous and he's got so much money stashed away he doesn't know what to do with it all. He even feels the tiniest bit guilty about having so much when others are hard-up for cash. Then one day he happens to hear about a girl who's starting up a riding centre out in the country, one specially to helped crippled children. It rings a bell. Maybe a long time ago he had some physical disability himself. But it's my bet that it takes him right back to the days when he was a barefoot country boy, riding to a little school in the back-blocks.'

'That was before he had any ideas of becoming a business tycoon?'

'Oh, definitely! He's a self-made character, a rough diamond. At least, that's how I imagine him. I think he wants to be in on helping the centre along. But you see in spite of being such a business success, he's shy about giving things. He likes to do his good works in secret——'

'Maybe his wife doesn't approve——'

'Oh no, he's not married. Not Mr. X!'

'You seem awfully sure about it.'

'Oh, I am!'

'Tempted?'

She laughed, the soft throaty laugh with a catch in it. 'No, I'll keep him just the way he is, bless his kind heart! But I've been so lucky. I've had so much help from folks around here. You've no idea how good everyone's been. Malcolm's father sent around a couple of ponies and they're ideal. No bad habits, the right age too. A bit overweight, but that's only because of lack of exercise——'

The deep tones broke across her excited tones. 'So now you're away! No more problems!'

'You've got to be joking! Problems—they're just endless!' Her voice sobered. 'And the biggest one of the lot is finance. Now I've got things started I've just got to keep the school running. It's my big chance. I make a small charge to each child of ten dollars for the course of lessons, then if they wish they can keep on afterwards when the course is finished. I have to charge something to keep going and of course if a child's parents can't afford the money I would take him just the same. I'm hoping that a lot of the children will be sponsored by a private person or a firm.'

'I get it. Any ideas about fund-raising?'

'Have I ever?' Liz stared ahead at the curve of lighted roadway unfolding ahead in the arc of the headlamps. Around them the trees were a dark mass, the only sound the whirring of tyres on the rough metal, the call of a nightbird in the bush. She had been speaking faster than usual in her low husky tones, in an effort to counteract the distracting intimacy of this small enclosed space cut off from the dark world outside. All the time she was aware of a disturbing masculine magnetism against which she had struggled from the first moment of their meeting. *Remember he's in love with someone else, and has been for years!* The thought gave her a moment of calmness, and she pulled her flyaway thoughts back to sanity, forced herself to speak more slowly. 'I thought . . . some publicity would help a lot. You know? Radio, newspapers, TV. Once folk get to know about what's happening up here they might get interested and feel like helping things along a bit. If not with money then maybe they'd offer their time or services. It's worth a try, wouldn't you say?'

He nodded carelessly. 'It might work at that!'

They swept in sight of the cottage. Evelyn had left a porch lantern burning, but everywhere else the place was in darkness.

'Hey, where are we going?' Liz turned a surprised face towards him as they sped past the long driveway and continued along the winding road. Her eyes were fixed on the lighted portion of highway ahead.

'Just for a ride. I thought you might care to take a look at the view from the cliff when the moon's rising over the water?'

'From your place, you mean?'

'Not so far away as that. There's a spot up on the cliffs, about half way between. You'll see in a minute——'

Swiftly he took the bush-shadowed roads and presently they were lurching up a rough track threaded with tree roots. Now Liz could hear the crash and thunder of waves pounding in on a rugged coast far below. It wasn't until she got out of the car, however, and he guided her along a narrow path at the cliff-edge that she caught her first view of the sea; moon-silvered waves washing in against a dramatic backdrop of dark hills, heavy with bush. Up here on the heights there was a a salty tang in the air and the strong wind from the sea swirled her long skirt around her, tearing at her topknot until the dark tendrils loosened and blew against her face. She turned towards him, laughing. 'You're right, Peter——' Odd how she felt this absurd hesitation about saying this one name and no other, 'it's really worth coming up here for.'

'*This* is what I came for!' He took a step towards her and some panicky impulse, an urge towards flight impelled her to take a quick step backwards, dislodging small stones that went bouncing and tumbling down hundreds of feet to the sands far below. In a second he was at her side, clasping her firmly, guiding her away from the dangerous edge, and at his touch ... his touch ...

'Trembling, Liz?'

'I ... got a fright,' she said huskily. 'Heights give me a funny feeling. I've no head for them, I guess.' He was still holding her and she knew that the sensation affecting her wasn't due to heights at all but to something else, something that was really a lot more dangerous. The next moment she felt his arms tighten around her, drawing her close, and a wild sweet happiness quivered along her nerves. She heard his deep soft laugh, then the waves of a great sea rose around her, drowning out everything else in the world but excitement and ecstasy.

At last he released her and immediately came the thought that spoilt it all. Liz Kennedy, a funny kid, something amusing with her odd schemes and dreams, someone to kiss ... when Beryl wasn't around to see! Trembling still, she flung herself away, hating him, hating herself. Oh, damn everything, she thought furiously. Wrenching herself from his outstretched hand, she stumbled back towards the car. 'I'd better get back,' she said breathlessly. 'Evelyn will be wondering where I am.'

When she glanced back he hadn't moved but stood motionless by the cliff edge, looking after her.

'Does it matter?'

Liz pretended she hadn't heard him as she opened the car door and slipped inside.

He took his time to join her, then without a word he put the vehicle in gear and they took the rough path back to the main road. It seemed to Liz no time at all until they were turning in at the entrance to the cottage. The moon was rising now, softening the outlines of the shabby house, flooding the grass with silver. At the foot of the steps he cut the engine and leaning back in his seat, studied her reflectively.

'I've got to hand it to you, Liz. You're doing fine. Keep it up!'

The deep intentness of his look, the timbre of his

voice as if somehow he *really* cared, almost betrayed her. If she didn't *know* how things were between him and Beryl ... Clutching wildly at her flying senses, Liz said the first thing that came into her mind. 'You don't care then about my being here, starting up a school on the property?'

'Care?' He stared at her in surprise. 'Why should I?'

'Oh, I don't know.' Liz nibbled a long strand of hair that had escaped from her topknot in the sea breeze. 'Just that I got the idea,' she stammered, avoiding that bright enquiring gaze, 'that you wanted the place for yourself ... you know, for water supply and beach access and all that.'

'And you imagined I'd stand in your way simply because of that trouble I had with the guy who had the place before you came? You thought *that*?'

'Well ...' She wanted to remind him that he hadn't been exactly helpful, apart from offering her a ride to the saleyards. Nor had he exhibited any special enthusiasm on learning of her plans for the centre, but the words stuck in her throat. It was difficult to think clearly when he was so close to her and the singing excitement was back in the summer night.

'Liz, look at me!' A hand cupped beneath her small square chin forced her to meet his gaze. Only for a second, then the firm lips were seeking her mouth and once again she was submerged in a high tide of heady excitement. At last she drew herself away. What was this? Madness to feel this way about a man who belonged to someone else! 'It's late,' she murmured unsteadily. 'Thanks for bringing me home.'

'But, Liz——'

Avoiding his detaining hand, she slipped away, and it wasn't until much later as she turned restlessly from side to side in bed that she realised she had won no victory over him after all. On the contrary, there had been moments tonight when she had been perilously close to giving him a victory over her! She had been in real danger of falling in love with a man who no doubt regarded her as someone new and different in this girl-scarce district. Impulsive, outspoken, fun to be with . . . for a time. But when it came to love . . . Beryl's flawless features rose in her mind and it seemed to her that the pale eyes mocked her.

CHAPTER 6

In the days that followed Liz was kept occupied with a variety of tasks. There were saddles to be cleaned and oiled, ponies to be inspected daily, and she really must get around to patching the torn canvas horse-covers on the old sewing machine Evelyn had put at her disposal. An empty box in the shed was still waiting to be stocked with supplies of oils and leather dressings, Stockholm tar, embrocation and various disinfectants.

One evening she was seated at the desk in the barn, endeavouring to compose an article dealing with the riding centre for submission to the editor of a national women's magazine. Half an hour later, after endless crossings-out and re-writing, she sat nibbling her pen. Who would have thought that the putting together of a few hundred words on a subject that was of such deep interest to her could present such difficulties? Yet somehow she must find the words to let the public know of her urgent need for funds with which to carry on her venture—explain how urgently she needed helpers who would give their time and services on regular visits to the riding centre. She had completed only one sheet of writing when she realised she had no photographs of ponies or grounds with which to illustrate her account of the disabled children, and the benefits they would receive from their hitherto unknown mobility. Well, the article would simply have to wait until she could snap some pictures on her Instamatic on the next visit of the children. She rose, stretching, then stood motionless, listening to the peal of the doorbell that was shrilling through the cottage. It might be Peter! Why did her thoughts fly instantly to him? Why was he in her mind practically all the day and half the night? Since the night of the dance when he had taken her to the clifftop she hadn't seen him, but ever since she found herself listening for his step, the sound of his voice. How *could* a kiss make everything so different?

The doorbell rang again. Evidently Evelyn and Stan were watching television in the house and hadn't heard the summons, for the next minute she caught the sound of approaching footsteps.

'Miss Kennedy!' Lewis Ridgway, immaculate in his light-weight summer suit, stood at the entrance. 'May I?' He smiled and moved towards her, his shoes ringing on the bare floorboards.

'Hello!' Liz was still feeling surprised to see him here, surprised ... and disappointed.

'I should have rung you and let you know I was on the way——' He swung himself up on a high stool facing her. 'The only excuse I've got is that I had a lot on my mind at the office today, and anyway,' he smiled again, 'I was fairly certain I'd be lucky enough to find you in.'

'That's right. I'm usually around the place.' All at once her tone sharpened. 'Julie? There's nothing wrong, is there?'

'Good grief no! She's her old happy self! You know Julie. Right now she's busy counting the days until the next riding day comes up.'

'Thank goodness!' Liz breathed out a sigh of relief. 'For one awful moment I wondered ... Would you care for some coffee? It's on the perk. It's a long drive out here from town on the winding roads in the dark.'

'Wonderful!'

While she busied herself with the percolator he glanced idly down at the desk, his gaze resting on the sheet of paper with its crossed-out paragraphs. 'What's this?'

'Oh, just an article I was trying to put together,' she was reaching down two beakers from the hooks above the table. 'If you could call it an article! Would you believe that those few paragraphs have taken me ages to think up and it still doesn't read like anything that's worth a second glance.'

'You won't mind if I run an eye over it?'

'Mind? I'd be delighted!'

Taking the steaming beaker of coffee she was extending towards him, he scanned the sheet of handwriting.

'It's okay,' he pronounced at last. 'I'd better admit right away that this is just what I had in mind when I came up here to see you tonight. Had a thought that all this is more in my line of country than yours, seeing that running an advertising outfit happens to be my game! If it's all right with you we could draft something out for the newspapers. One or two of the local magazines run this type of article too. I'll get my secretary to run them off in the morning. What do you say?'

'Oh, *would* you?' Liz felt almost as pleased as though the unknown Mr. X had sent her a second thousand-dollar cheque in the mail for the benefit of the fund.

'Leave it to me. If you don't mind I'll work from this page of yours. It gives all the data, fills in on the main points, the general idea of the riding centre.' His grey eyes were thoughtful, abstracted. 'Now about the newspapers. I know the editors of the two main city papers. I'll give them a ring in the morning and they can send out reporters to get the story. They could cover the riding lesson next week. Okay?'

She nodded eagerly, hands clasped around her beaker of coffee. 'Oh, that would be fabulous! You've no idea what a relief it is to have the whole thing taken out of my hands! It's awfully good of you to go to all this trouble——'

'I'd like to do a lot more than that, for *you*.' She barely caught the low words and at her puzzled glance he made a gesture with outspread well-shaped hands. 'Forget it ... just a long-term project of mine.' All at once his tone was once again businesslike, impersonal. 'Now about advertising the place, getting yourself known. Radio reaches a lot more folk than you'd think, actually. Just happens that I'm in touch with the chief of the main station, so there won't be any problems there. We should get results almost right away.'

At the clipped confident tones Liz eyed him in amazement. 'You do seem to know an awful lot of influential people.'

He nodded carelessly. 'It helps, especially when you want to get something off the ground in a hurry! Saves all the messing about and wasting time.' His tone was that of a man accustomed to organising, to giving orders to subordinates. 'I'll get cracking on this first thing tomorrow. Three magazine articles ... that means you'll need some pictures to send along with them to grab public interest.'

Liz's face fell. 'If only I'd thought to take some snaps of the children when they were on the ponies. I could have had them processed by now. We could have got the articles ready for submission to the magazines right away. Some of them only publish once a month.'

'Not to worry. I took a few snaps myself that day,' Lewis said modestly. Taking a folder from his breast pocket he spread out on the desk a number of black and white prints. 'They're small, but they can be blown up easily enough.'

'Look, there's Julie!' Liz pounced on a picture of a radiant fair-haired girl. 'Did you ever see such a wonderful smile?'

'I know. With Julie happiness is a pony! She's a bright kid any time, but out here with you and the horses ... Here's one of Taiere. Only a small Maori boy could produce a monstrous grin like that! No fear there—he's enjoying every moment of it. He's getting the devil of a kick out of it. He looks as proud as though he were riding in the Melbourne Cup——'

Liz laughed. 'He probably was, and winning the race too. In between being a dashing cowboy, that is!' Her face sobered as she picked up another picture. 'Poor Danny. He's simply terrified, but he's brave too. He *made* himself get up there and take that ride.'

'Next time it won't come so hard, or the next——'

'I know, I know.'

'They'll do for a start.' He shuffled the pictures back

into a folder. 'Oh, something else too that nearly slipped my mind. I took a chance and contacted the TV boys about your project. They're sending out a camera team in two weeks' time. Seem to think the riding school would make a good news feature, so I'm hoping it may whip up a lot of public interest and a bit of financial support as well. One thing, at least you'll get some helpers out of it. By the way, the TV team are doing a riding commercial for some cosmetic outfit, helping along a new brand of make-up they're putting on the market. It goes under the name of Today's Girl——'

'I've never heard of it.'

'You will! Seems they're on the lookout for a riding background, somewhere not too far away; wanted to know if they could come up here and shoot some outdoor scenes. They told me to ask you if you'd be willing to do them a favour and let them film some shots of you on your chestnut——'

'But,' she stared across at him incredulously, 'they wouldn't want *me*!'

'Why wouldn't they? Ever done any TV work? Announcing, fashion modelling, advertising? That sort of stuff?'

She shook her head. 'Heavens, no, I'm not the type.'

'How do you know you're not? I'll tell you something, Miss Kennedy,' his voice was warm, enthusiastic. 'From what the TV boys told me I got the impression that you happen to be just the sort of girl they've got in mind for the particular commercial they want to film.'

Liz was scarcely listening. Fashion modelling? At last she knew the reason for the vague sense of familiarity Beryl had for her. It must be some years ago that the even features and superb figure had flashed across the tiny screen. Beryl holding a modern stance displaying the latest in sports gear, race-meeting fashions, glittering theatre gowns. All at once she realised Lewis had stopped short and was eyeing her curiously. 'What's the matter?'

'Nothing, nothing.' She switched her mind back to

the present and noticed with some surprise the sudden softening of his gaze.

'Thing is they're looking for a girl who's an outdoor type. Nothing fussy or glamorous, just a barefoot girl, hair blowing in the wind, out riding for the fun of it!'

Liz sent him a teasing smile. 'When you put it that way it does sound a bit like me.'

'That's what I'm trying to get through to you! Well, Miss Kennedy, what do you say?'

She hesitated, nibbling a long strand of dark hair in an unconscious gesture. 'I suppose ... if it's not a close-up ...'

'I wouldn't imagine so. What they're after is a country background shot of a girl taking a horse over a hurdle. "Give Life a Whirl with Today's Girl!" That sort of thing!'

'I've only got Red,' she murmured doubtfully, 'and he's a chestnut. Would be be all right, his colour I mean, for photography?'

'Sure! They said anything except a white horse would suit them fine. Told me to tell you to bleach his mane and tail, it's more effective to get some contrast into the picture.' Once again his tone softened. 'From what they said I got the idea that you'd be just about made to order for the part.'

'For goodness' sake!' She stared up at him.

'It's not *my* idea!' He smiled towards her. 'You need the money, don't you? Think how it would help the fund!'

'Oh yes, the fund! I'd forgotten all about that.' Suddenly her mind was made up. 'All right then, I'll do it!'

'You will? Great! I'd better warn you, though, that it's a rush job. Could you make it tomorrow, two o'clock?'

'You seem,' she said suspiciously, 'to have it all arranged for me already.'

'All but your say-so, Miss Kennedy!'

The slightly formal tone amused her and she said lightly. 'Isn't it about time you called me Liz, like everyone else?'

'If you'll make it Lewis——'

'It's a deal!'

'Let's shake on it!' The thin dark face was faintly flushed with pleasure as he caught her hand in his. 'I'm beginning to see why young Julie thinks the sun rises and sets in you!' Liz wondered if he had forgotten to release her small brown paw. The next moment some instinct of being observed drew her glance towards the doorway where a tall shadowy figure stood silhouetted against the opening. He was motionless, the tip of a lighted cigarette a scarlet glow against the darkness outside. 'Hi, Liz!' Did she imagine an ironical note in the deep, well-remembered tones? And how long had he been standing there, taking in the little scene of the two seated at the desk, hands in a lingering clasp?

'Peter!' Wrenching her hand away, she leaped to her feet. 'Did you want to see me?'

But already he was turning away. 'Sorry, can't stay. I just brought you something ... left it with Stan.' As she continued to stare after him bewilderedly, he threw over his shoulder: 'Something you said you wanted. You'll see.'

She made a wild guess. 'It's not—you didn't bring McGinty?' she cried delightedly.

'He's a bit on the small side for McGinty, better make it Mac. Sorry, I've got to get cracking. See you around.'

She moved back into the lighted room, all her previous enthusiasm in the matter of arranging publicity for the riding school forgotten. If only she hadn't been involved here tonight with Lewis Ridgway! If only Peter had chosen to come another night, any other night, rather than this particular one! All at once she became aware of Lewis's intent glance. 'Friend of yours?' he enquired sharply.

'No, no,' she sank back on the stool, endeavouring to gather together her whirling thoughts. 'Just a neighbour. Now where were we?'

'Just about packed up for tonight, I'd say.' He was

collecting papers, putting them into a leather folder. A few moments later, after thanking her with old-fashioned courtesy for the coffee, he left her to drive away.

Even before the twin red tail lamps of the opulent-looking car had been swallowed up on the winding road, Liz was running down the broken pathway towards a pale blur in the darkness of the paddock that she just knew would be McGinty. Sure enough as she came nearer she made out a kid with soft long hair and a stubby tail. 'McGinty! Mac! Come here!' As if already familiar with his name the tiny creature moved towards her and Liz cradled him in her arms. What a pet he would be for the children, and how they would revel in the feel of his silky coat. If only she'd been free tonight to thank Steve for bringing him to her.

'Will he do?' Her pulses leaped as Peter, accompanied by Stan, strolled around a corner of the shed. While the older man went back to the cottage, Peter strolled towards her.

'Oh, he's just a darling!' She put the kid down on the dew-wet grass and turned to face him. 'I—I thought you'd gone,' she heard herself say inanely.

'I should have,' he leaned an elbow on the slip-rails, 'but Stan wanted some advice on a building project he's working on for the boss——'

'Oh, that would be the new ramp he's going to make for me——'

'You've certainly got things under control around here, Liz,' his laconic tone sharpened. 'What did Ridgway want?'

'Lewis? Do you know him?'

He shrugged. 'Only by sight. I've seen his picture in the papers often enough. I gather he's the brains of the country's leading advertising outfit. The sort of guy who could help you a whole lot in that direction if he wanted to—*does* he want to?'

In the starshine she couldn't glimpse his expression, but there was no mistaking the satirical tone. She wished he wouldn't shoot questions at her in this peremptory way, questions that seemed to hint at a lot more than the mere words conveyed.

'I scarcely know him really. He's just interested in the riding school because of his daughter——'

'I didn't say he wasn't! You *are* touchy tonight, Liz!'

'I am not!' How had she got herself involved in this absurd argument? 'It was just ... the way you said it.' She glanced down at McGinty, who had apparently attached herself to the enemy, said defensively, 'He's been awfully good about arranging publicity for the centre. He's really going to get it known about.' She paused and in the silence she was sure he was mocking her. 'He's getting reporters to come out and feature the place in the local newspapers,' she ran wildly on, 'and he's arranging for shots to be taken for a TV programme.'

'Good for you, Liz!' The ironic tone made her wonder. Was he laughing at her once again? She wished she knew. Confusion made her add for something to say to break the silence: 'He told me the producers are looking for a riding school background and a girl to match. Seems it's a commercial they want to make, something to do with a product called "Today's Girl". They're sending a camera team up here tomorrow,' she ran on breathlessly. 'Isn't it ridiculous? Me!'

'I wouldn't think so.' Now she was glad of the soft darkness, certain that at this moment he was regarding her with a mocking glint in those lively hazel eyes. 'I think you'd feature quite well under that heading.'

'It's not a heading,' Liz protested unhappily, confusedly. Why must he discuss her as though she were a commodity, or a feature, or something of the sort? 'It's advertising for a line of cosmetics. Silly, isn't it, when I scarcely ever use any.'

'That's why you'd be just the one for it!'

To get him away from the subject of herself, she heard her own voice saying. 'Have you ever watched a TV commercial being made? They'll be here at two tomorrow afternoon——' Oh heavens, now he would think she was building herself up, boasting. 'If you'd care to come along?'

'I can hardly wait.'

Now she knew he was mocking her. 'Well, anyway,' she said awkwardly, 'thanks for bringing Mac over. He'll be a real favourite with the children and he'll be great for the ponies too. Get them used to other animals and sudden movements, all that sort of thing.'

'Glad he's what you wanted.' He spoke off-handedly. 'See you tomorrow—Today's Girl!' He swung around and moved towards the car standing in the driveway, leaving Liz with a niggling sense of unease. What had caused his sudden change of attitude towards her since the night of the dance? The two suppositions that flashed through her mind were each too utterly ridiculous to consider seriously. For how could Peter be jealous of Lewis Ridgway, jealous because of *her*? And for that matter, how could a kiss matter to him, a man already in love with another girl?

If only she hadn't blurted out the matter of the TV commercial. Now he would feel himself duty bound to come out here tomorrow whether he really wanted to or not. And the answer was probably the latter. How humiliating to remember that any day now Peter would give Beryl a token of their love in the form of a glittering engagement ring. For Liz Kennedy she brought McGinty! Somehow it wasn't even funny. She sighed and moved slowly towards the lighted cottage.

In anticipation of her afternoon engagement with the TV cameramen Liz took unusual care with her dressing, pressing crumpled blue jeans and mending the torn buttonholes in her white cotton blouse. Seeing that there had been mention of a barefoot rider her lack of respectable jodhpur boots wouldn't matter. It wouldn't be strictly a riding photograph, of course, not strictly anything, but still ... She washed her hair and seated herself on the top step at the back door of the cottage, while the hot sunshine sparked reddish lights in the black strands. All at once she paused, gazing down towards the house paddock. This morning McGinty had been there, safe and sound. Now he was nowhere to be seen. A swift search of the area confirmed her suspicions. Small and agile, he had pushed beneath a loose wire of the fence and made his escape. Liz couldn't understand why she felt so suddenly bereft. All at once it seemed awfully important that she find McGinty before Peter arrived here today. The trouble was, she realised almost right away, that a small white animal was difficult to distinguish.

She searched for an hour without success. There were so many paddocks and small patches of bush where McGinty could be hidden from sight. At last she went up the path, searching among the overhanging shrubs on either side and calling his name. When she reached the road she went scuffling along in the dust at the side of the rough metal, glancing around her as she went on. She must have moved a hundred yards or so when a flash of white among a tangle of flax and fern not far from the roadside alerted her. McGinty was reaching up to nibble at a blackberry bush above his head. She tried to creep silently up behind him and take him by surprise, but the snap of a small twig betrayed her and, jerked to sudden awareness, the kid leaped ahead. Liz leaped too, landing on her stomach among the blackberries, but she scarcely felt the prickles, for she was clasping McGinty triumphantly by a leg and hauling him through the undergrowth. At last she jerked the struggling animal into her arms and pushing her way through closely-growing fern and tea-tree, she emerged in sight of the road. A familiar car was approaching and Beryl waved from the driver's seat, then braked to a stop. The other girl gazed towards Liz's flushed face. 'What on earth——?'

'It was McGinty.' Her voice died away beneath the cool amused stare from the pale eyes. Faced with Beryl's flawless perfection all at once Liz was discomfitingly aware of her own dishevelled appearance. Swiftly she recovered herself and floundered on, 'He got out of his paddock and I had such a time finding him, but I caught him in the end!'

'Hop in!' Sandy flung open a rear door and Liz, still clinging firmly to a struggling McGinty, squeezed in the back seat between the silver-haired woman and the lad who she had already seen at the local dance. The small sulky face was turned to Liz in obvious amusement. 'You look funny. You've got grass in your hair!'

'So would you, if you'd chased a kid all through the bush!' Liz felt hot and sticky with paspalum grass and she had just noticed that purple berries she had contacted in her fall to the ground during her wild dash after McGinty had squashed down the front of her one presentable blouse, with disastrous results. A further dismaying thought struck her. 'You weren't on your way here for a riding lesson today, were you, Darryl?'

'That's right. Did you forget? Only it's not a lesson, it's a ride.' He sent her a contemptuous glance from beneath heavy lids. 'I don't have lessons. That's kid's stuff!'

Liz brushed back long hair from a heated forehead. 'Don't you believe it!' she said with asperity. 'You'd be surprised at the number of grown men who take riding lessons, even though they may have been riding for years.'

Sandy turned a backward glance towards Liz. 'Just what I've been trying to get through to him all week.'

'Me, I'm all for children having confidence in themselves,' Beryl was swinging the car in at the opening of the driveway. 'The way I see it it's far more important for Darryl to have faith in his own ability to ride a horse than being taught a lot of stuff that doesn't matter a scrap!'

'Aren't you forgetting something?' Sandy argued as they moved down the drive. 'A little matter of self-preservation? If he's going to get on a horse at all he should be taught the fundamentals of how to handle his mount. That is, if he isn't going to take a header on to the ground one of these days.'

'Oh, Sandy!' Beryl braked and turned towards him, the beautifully curving lips parted in a mocking smile. 'On these ancient nags? You've got to be joking!'

'I'm not, you know,' he persisted in his quiet serious tones. 'Even a quiet-tempered pony can get a fright at something that looms up on the roadway and take off, bolt with the rider when he least expects it——'

Soft pink lips pouted. 'You're so *hard*, Sandy! You don't seem to understand Darryl at all.'

His mouth was a hard line. 'We've had all this out before. It's only for his own good that I'm telling you. I know what I'd do if he were my lad——'

'Well, he's not, is he?' She gave a short angry laugh. 'Or likely to be!'

Sandy was silent.

'I'm not riding any crummy old pony!' Darryl cried rebelliously. 'You wouldn't have got me to come here at all if I'd known I had to get up on one of those dopes!' Imperiously he pointed towards Red, standing quietly within the tea-tree bars of the corral. 'I'll have the chestnut! That one over there!'

'Sorry,' Liz was polite but firm, 'but he happens to be Red, my show-jumper. He's only suitable for experienced riders.' She added smilingly, 'You don't want to have to bail out in a hurry, do you?'

'I wouldn't do that!' The boastful tones rang with self-confidence. 'I could handle him ... easy!'

Liz, however, was accustomed to dealing with difficult children. 'Later on when you've had a few lessons maybe I'll think about letting you have Red ... *maybe*. But for a start everyone has to have a quiet mount.' She reached a hand towards the door handle. 'You can take Cobber——'

'Thank you for nothing!' The boy's mouth was set in a sulky curve. 'I'm not riding any stupid little pony. Beryl,' he appealed to his stepmother, 'you said I could have a decent horse if I came here!'

'I'll go and put McGinty back in his paddock.' Calmly disregarding the whining tones, Liz got out of the door Sandy was holding open for her. At that moment Stan came to join them. He smiled towards the group and taking the kid from Liz said, 'So you found him! I'll attend to him for you.'

'Thanks, Stan. Darryl's come for a ride. If you'll just wait here,' she called over her shoulder to the group, 'I'll go and fetch Cobber. Won't be long!'

Together she and Stan went down the path and in a

few minutes Liz returned leading a thin grey pony while Stan went to the shed to collect sheepskin and saddle.

Ignoring Darryl's petulant expression, Liz led the pony forward.

'Here he is,' she said cheerfully, throwing over the pony's back the white fluffy sheepskin. She fitted the saddle and bent to fasten the girth. 'He's the biggest of the ponies we have here.'

'Ha, ha!' The lad tossed back lank fair hair in an insolent gesture. 'If that old nag's the biggest you've got on the place—— Look at him! You can see his bones! Don't you feed your horses around here?'

At the contemptuous curl of the boy's lips Liz controlled her rising anger with an effort. In a brief flashback she had a sudden vision of another lad of much the same age, who too had taken his first ride on one of these ponies, a ride that had called for every ounce of determination Danny had possessed; that had meant a battle against almost insurmountable obstacles. Crushing down her rising indignation and the disgust that filled her, she forced herself to say calmly, 'Come here. I'll give you a leg up.'

A little awed by the unmistakable note of authority in the soft tones, Darryl swaggered towards her.

'The other side when you mount a horse, please, Darryl!'

'Aw, I know.' With an attempt at bravado he hitched his hipster belt with its great chased silver buckle and after many awkward attempts, at last managed to haul himself up into the saddle.

'Now remember,' Liz told him firmly, 'you hold the reins so—no, not like that! This is the way. Don't hold on to Cobber's mane, you're not to rely on that. Knees in, close to the pony's sides. Back straight . . . straighter than that! Now I'll lead you up to the gate and back.'

'I'm not gonna be led, like a baby. Everyone'll see me!'

Disregarding the whining tones, Liz set off up the path. 'It's the same for everyone. Later on when you get more used to riding you can take Cobber along the road by yourself, but not today.'

'Aw, heck . . .'

For an instant, as she led the pony past the watching group Liz met the glance of Sandy McPhail. Taking in the angry expression of the strong face, the tightened lips, she guessed that he too was having difficulty in restraining his feelings. But what was the use? He had no authority over the boy. Darryl was in Beryl's care and she seemed bent on indulging him in every way possible, regardless of the damage being done to his character.

Liz led the pony to the front entrance and back to the car. 'You can take Cobber into the paddock by the house now,' she told the boy. 'Remember you're not to take him out of a walk. Now turn——'

With a cruel jerk of the reins he pulled the pony towards a small gate. Liz waited there to open it, and closed it after him. 'You understand, Darryl? You're not to ride anywhere but in the paddock!'

'Okay, okay, you told me.'

As she went back to join the others she reflected that it was useless to attempt to teach the boy anything of the principles of riding correctly. He had already made up his mind that he knew it all, and to cause an open argument wouldn't help anyone. It was a cheering thought, she reflected, that after this one experience of riding she probably wouldn't be troubled with him again.

'You don't have to *watch* me!' called the rebellious voice from the paddock. But of course they did, eyeing Darryl as he urged the pony round and round in continuous circles on the grass until Liz thought that Cobber must surely be feeling giddy. At length she strolled towards the boy. 'Had enough riding yet?'

'Call this riding?' he scoffed. 'If you'd let me go out on the road I'd show you. I'd zoom along . . . whee! Nothing to it!' The bragging voice followed Liz as she went to open the gate. 'Back in Queensland where I come from there are ranches that would make this dump look like nothing at all.'

'Right, that'll do for today. I've got another

119

appointment in a few minutes.'

'Another one?' Darryl eyed her in surprise. 'Is there someone else coming for a lesson?'

'Not exactly. I'm the rider this time.' Liz spoke without thinking. 'It's a TV camera team, actually——' She glanced up towards the empty road winding over the hills.

'Gee!' Darryl's voice held a new respectful note.

Beryl, who had strolled across the grass to meet them, was also eyeing Liz with interest. For once she appeared to have abandoned her customary supercilious attitude towards her and was saying eagerly. 'Did I hear you say that a TV team is coming here today to do some filming?'

'Uh-huh.' Liz was helping Darryl to dismount. 'Seems they want a riding background for a commercial they're producing. Some cosmetic thing. Heavens!' she glanced down at her wrist-watch, 'I'll have to fly! They'll be here in a moment and my blouse ... I'll simply have to change!'

She turned to find Sandy at her side. 'Let me put the pony back in the paddock.' Already he was taking the reins from her hands. 'You zip inside and freshen up.' He smiled towards her and added in his steady tones, 'Don't worry, Miss Kennedy, we'll hold them at bay until you get back.'

'Oh, we'll do more than that!' All at once Beryl was gay and animated. 'Isn't it the luckiest thing,' she cried in her high tones, 'my just happening to be here today! To think I only came because of Darryl pestering me to have a ride——'

'You mean,' enquired her aunt in her hesitant way, 'because of your TV experience?'

'What else? You see,' she explained to Liz with unaccustomed friendliness, 'I've had oodles of experience in television acting.' She raised an exquisitely manicured hand to touch a cloud of silver-gilt hair. 'I've been told a hundred times that natural blonde colouring like mine is perfect for photography. So if they're wanting a girl to feature in the commercial, well ...' The smile she flashed around the group spelled the message out clearly. Beauty, talent, experience, what more could anyone want in a television advertisement?

Olga said: 'Here they come now.'

Liz too had caught the sound of an approaching station waggon. Hurrying to her room, she rummaged wildly through her bureau drawers in search of a clean blouse. She found one at last. It was hopelessly crumpled, but there was no time to use the iron, for already voices reached her from outside the window. Liz was aware of one voice in particular, feminine, high, argumentative. She dragged the blouse over her head, popping off a button in the process. No matter, she would just have to hope no one would notice. She flew out of the door.

Despite her haste she saw at once that the cameramen were already adjusting their cameras. She hurried towards them. 'Sorry I'm late!' She was still breathless as she gestured towards the small knot of onlookers. 'Do you all know each other?'

'Now we do!' A tall thin young man with a drooping brown moustache eyed her consideringly. 'You're Miss Kennedy?'

She nodded smilingly and his fellow-worker, an older man with a pleasant freckled face, moved towards her. 'Hope you can oblige us with some pictures today, Miss Kennedy?'

Liz said doubtfully, 'Yes, of course ... if you still want me?'

The keen eyes of the younger cameraman raked her hesitant face. 'What's all this about not wanting you? Is there something wrong? We only want a few shots ... won't keep you long.'

'No, no, it's not that. It's just that I thought you might prefer to have someone more—well, professional. You see, Mrs. Manners has had a lot of experience before the cameras. You might remember her work on TV?'

'Before my time, I'm afraid,' the man with the brown moustache replied carelessly. All at once Liz realised that Beryl was pale, her lips pressed firmly together. Clearly the other girl was very, very angry.

'I've met Mrs. Manners somewhere,' the older cameraman's tone was smooth and conciliatory, 'but can't think where. Wait, I've got it! Wasn't it at a fashion show that was televised on an overseas liner in port at the time, in Auckland, a few years ago?'

'Yes.' Beryl appeared to have some difficulty in getting the word out. Liz couldn't help thinking that the blue eyes appeared to be paler than ever, as though the colour were washed out of them, or was that just because of the bleakness of Beryl's expression?

'Too bad we couldn't make use of you today,' the freckled-faced man was squinting into the lens, testing camera angles, 'but you see how it is. We have to consider the sponsors, seeing they're the ones who are footing the bill, and with a make-up with a tag like To-day's Girl——'

'What do you mean?' Beryl's voice was ominously quiet. 'Are you telling me that I'm not——'

'Oh, don't get me wrong, Mrs. Manners. You'd be fine for the usual type of commercial.' The cameramen, obviously enmeshed in a delicate situation, was feeling his way with care. Liz thought he could scarcely have escaped the impact of Beryl's icy stare. 'But it just happens that for this commercial we're looking for a certain type ... just a girl with a happy smile ... free ... high-spirited, *young*. I guess Ridgway was right when he told us that the girl he'd found had no need to play the part, she was ready-made!' All at once his face cleared and on an inspiration he added: 'Of course what we're looking for is a girl who can ride like the wind, sail over a high jump, take a farm fence in her stride!'

'Oh, that's different, then!' It was obvious to everyone that Beryl was grasping eagerly at the proffered opportunity to escape from an intolerably humiliating situation. It must surely be the single occasion in the other girl's life, Liz thought, when Beryl had been denied something she really wanted. 'Of course if that's the way it is, I really couldn't consider the part.'

'That's what I thought,' the cameraman answered

smoothly. 'Now, if you'll just move out of the way?' He turned towards Liz. 'Ready, Miss Kennedy?'

'I haven't any proper riding gear——'

'Who the devil cares about that?' he answered warmly. 'Today's Girl doesn't, and that's for sure.' (So he wasn't particularly concerned about her crumpled denim blouse, Liz thought with relief). She brought her mind back to the quick tones. 'What if she doesn't wear conventional gear for riding? She couldn't care less about that sort of thing. She's got an air of living every moment to the full, she lets her hair blow loose in the wind and when she takes her mount over a high jump, she enjoys it as much as he does! Get the picture?'

She laughed. 'As long as you're happy about it.' At least, she reflected, Red was carefully groomed, for she had brushed the chestnut coat to a silky gleam, combed the long pale mane and tail.

While the men made final adjustments to their cameras, Stan went to the paddock to fetch Red. But when the chestnut appeared, coat gleaming in the sunlight, mane and tail newly bleached to a pale cream shade, someone else was leading him. Liz felt her heart plunge. For Peter was leading the mount towards her and as she met the special smile he seemed to keep for her, suddenly the scene around her became dazzlingly clear and sharp, a moment she knew that would be for ever etched in memory.

He helped her to mount. 'Good luck, Liz!' For a moment he held her gaze, then with an effort of will she wrenched her glance aside. 'Thanks, Peter.'

As she guided Red towards the gate opening into a wide paddock, Darryl cried: 'Wait a minute! She hasn't got a saddle! And that jump looks hangofa high!'

The younger cameraman grinned towards him. 'Leave that to us, son. Miss Kennedy doesn't look too worried and if she's happy seated on an old sugar sack—okay with you, Miss Kennedy, if we have the jump raised a bit? The higher the better for the picture, if you get us?'

123

She nodded and turned to Peter. 'Will you——'

He raised the red and white pole that Stan had erected in the side paddock for the occasion. 'Right! You're away!'

Liz urged Red forward and he moved off with his long easy canter. Liz's hair streamed behind her, then the jump loomed up and she felt Red gather himself for the leap. Crouching forward, she felt the big chestnut stretch himself out over the rails, clearing the high bar with inches to spare.

'Fine!' The freckled-faced photographer sounded pleased. 'Now for another!' Once again she set her mount to the jump and Red flew effortlessly over the bars.

'Was it all right?' she called.

'Tremendous!' The younger cameraman shot her a swift enquiring glance. 'How would you feel about one more shot, with the jump raised higher still?'

She was giving the chestnut an appreciative pat. 'No trouble to Red.'

'Right!' Once again Peter raised the bar.

'Here we go!' She touched the horse's side with a bare foot, gripping with her knees as Red cantered towards the painted rail. She was aware of the strong muscles beneath her flexing and as always at this moment when Red took off the ground, excitement gripped her. Blue sky and green paddocks rocketed together, then all too soon it was over. Liz circled the paddock, then, flushed and smiling, she pulled up at the side of the watching group.

'Will that do? Have you enough pictures now?'

'Thanks, yes, Miss Kennedy. We took plenty of shots. Just what we were looking for, eh, Alec?' The younger man appealed to his co-worker. 'The right girl in the right set-up! With this bright sunshine I reckon we've got some sharp pictures——' All at once he appeared to remember Beryl, standing silently a short distance away. 'We might be calling on you one of these days, Mrs. Manning, If you're still interested in TV work?'

For a second a gleam flickered in the frozen blue

eyes. 'Any time. You'll find my telephone number in the book.'

'Right! We'll be in touch.'

As the photographer turned away, Bery glanced towards Liz with such unmistakable malice that Liz knew that unwittingly she had made an enemy. Previously she had sensed in the other girl an attitude of careless contempt, but now jealousy and dislike flared in her glance.

'We'll be out next week to get some shots of the handicapped kids on their ponies——' Liz became aware of the cameraman's voice. 'That is, if it's okay with you, Miss Kennedy?'

'Yes, of course.'

'We're always looking for good news items, and this riding outfit of yours for the disabled kids sounds like something that would catch the public interest. Right now we've got to get back to the studio. 'Bye!' His cheerful wave included the group of watchers standing in the paddock.

From a corner of her eye Liz realised that Peter too was leaving. For a moment he paused beside her and she was at once agonisingly conscious of his nearness. There was no doubt of the pleased expression in his eyes. 'Congratulations, Liz. I'll be watching out for you on the screen!' With a parting grin he turned away. The next minute Beryl was running after him, calling in her high carrying tones, 'Pete! You'll be over for cocktails tonight? You promised——'

'Sure.' Liz watched him get into his car and as the vehicle shot up the drive somehow for her the excitement of the afternoon faded. Was it because of the other girl's timely reminder that so far as Liz was concerned, Peter Farraday was merely a slightly interested neighbour, *nothing more*, that she felt this sudden sense of let-down?

While Stan led the chestnut away, Liz moved in the direction of the cottage. She hadn't realised that others too had made their way there until feminine voices echoed from the open window of the kitchen.

'Thanks, Beryl dear.' Olga's slightly apologetic tones

125

floated through the clear air. 'I was dying for a drink of water,' the wistful voice ran on, 'but I just couldn't bear to tear myself away. I was fascinated watching that girl taking those high jumps, and looking so care-free and happy about it. I do think it's marvellous what Miss Kennedy's doing for all those handicapped children. I mean, it must be costing her the earth, and she gets nothing out of it!'

'Oh, Olga, don't be so naïve!' Beryl's forceful tones came clearly to the girl strolling up the path. 'You don't really think she's doing it all just for the sake of the kids?'

'Well, isn't she?'

Liz found herself pausing, listening in spite of her-self.

'For heaven's sake be your age! She's already got Lewis Ridgway eating out of her hand. A widower, one of the wealthiest and most influential men in the city ... great work, if you can get it! Oh, don't look at me like that! It's only what everyone will be saying pretty soon! And how about all those interesting doc-tors and specialists who are always around on the days the kids come out to get a ride?' The high tones were tinged with malice. 'Wonderful, Miss Kennedy! Keep up the good work, Miss Kennedy! We couldn't do without you, Miss Kennedy! It makes me *sick*! For a girl who's husband-hunting she can take her pick—if she plays her cards the right way! Why, even Peter——' Liz was holding her breath. 'Make no mis-take, she'd even get hold of him if she could!'

Liz felt a stab of almost physical pain. She didn't care what the other girl said about the others, but Peter ... that hurt, that *really* hurt, made her realise all over again how utterly hopeless it was for her to imagine she could mean anything in his life—ever. She became aware once more of the venomous tones. 'Any-one else would see what her game is in a minute, any-one but a silly sentimentalist like you!'

'I don't care what you say,' Olga's tones quivered but she stuck to her guns, 'I still think you're all wrong about her, Beryl!'

A laugh, short, bitter, without amusement. 'You would! You're as soft as butter! But you'll come around to my way of thinking one of these days. She's got Lewis Ridgway just where she wants him and if she can do that in one meeting—well, you'll see that I'm right ... and before too long either!'

'I don't believe that's all she's doing it for.'

Liz didn't wait to hear any more. She turned away and went blindly towards the barn. She scarcely knew or cared where she was, she only knew she couldn't, wouldn't meet Beryl Manning face to face at this minute. With a faint sense of surprise she noticed that her sun-tanned hand was visibly shaking. So this was the other girl's revenge for being overlooked by the TV team in favour of barefoot Liz Kennedy in her shabby denim shirt and jeans. How *could* she! But a jealous woman would say anything against a rival, especially one so indulged and pampered as Beryl. No doubt she would take pleasure in spreading those cruel lies around the district, lies that Liz would find difficulty in refuting. Could it be, the thought came unbidden, that Beryl had yet another reason for her black jealousy? Was it because out there in the sunshine a few minutes ago, Peter had looked at her with such pride and pleasure?

Only Olga had defended her. Liz could imagine the older woman's earnest, wistful face. She knew a moment's pity for her. Imagine having to live with that lovely, spiteful creature who was so utterly different in outlook from herself! Perhaps Olga was a poor relative, offered a holiday in the country in exchange for light household duties. But to be forced to be at the receiving end of Beryl's changing moods ... She sighed, thinking that if Peter were in love with her she'd be so happy she wouldn't ever say a cruel word to anyone. But of course Beryl was accustomed to having adulation, it was nothing to her. A girl like that would take it as her due. As to herself, she would do better to put her mind to other matters instead of dreaming the impossible dream.

Peter ... She stared unseeingly through a high window and for a moment the scene outside shimmered in a mist because of the moisture that clouded her eyes. It hurt, what Beryl had said about her and Peter, because it was the truth. She'd give anything for him to love her, *as she loved him*. There! She'd come right out with it. So ... one could love again ... only this time it was real. The other had been a brief physical attraction, a jolt to her pride, and that was all. But this ... and he belonged to Beryl. Even though she knew it was too late, even though nothing could ever come of it, she would go on loving him just the same, wanting him with this hopeless longing because she couldn't help herself. There was just nothing she could do about it.

CHAPTER 7

On Tuesday when the first ambulance nosed in at the driveway Liz was glad she had got up early and with Stan and Malcolm's help, had the ponies saddled and tied to the hitching rail in readiness for the children's arrival. Almost immediately a second ambulance appeared, followed by private cars and soon smiling St. John Ambulance drivers were placing wheelchairs on the grass. Children were carried towards them and crutches handed to those who could use them. In a matter of minutes the area was alive with sudden activity and an atmosphere of happiness and excitement pervaded the air.

'Miss Kennedy! Miss Kennedy!' Liz, talking with a young woman therapist, glanced around as a gleaming car pulled up at her side and a child's fair head was thrust from the window. She met Julie's infectious smile and laughing eyes.

'Here you are!' Liz pushed forward an empty wheelchair and Lewis lifted the small girl from the car and placed her in the chair. Wildly excited, Julie's small face was one smile of delight as Liz helped Lewis to lift the child up to the back of a small black pony. 'Pinocchio knows me!' she cried as Liz guided the helplessly hanging legs into special safety stirrups. 'He winked at me! What'll I do now, Miss Kennedy? This is my *real* lesson, isn't it?'

Lewis sent Liz a quizzical look, then shrugged his shoulders. 'She's wild with excitement! Suppose in a way you can't blame the kid!'

'It's something to be excited about, getting mobile all of a sudden!' Liz was fitting a riding cap over the blonde curls. 'Now first of all, Julie you've got to learn how to balance on Pinocchio——'

'What's balance?'

'Sitting up straight, feeling comfortable——'

'But I am!'

'So you are! You're wonderful!' For the child, relaxed and happy, showed no sign of apprehension. 'But there are a few things you must learn if you're going to be a good rider. Back straight——' She placed the reins in the small hands, 'hold on to these, not the pony's mane. Do you understand?'

Julie nodded eagerly. 'Look, Daddy, I'm riding!' A look of unbelievable pleasure and surprise crossed the small face. *'I'm higher than you!'*

'It's not fair,' her father complained, but a secret look passed between him and Liz—on her part a glance of satisfaction, on his an expression of delight that deepened to something warmer. Or was she imagining a special significance in his smile? Today he wore dark rectangular sunglasses and his expression escaped her. 'After that,' she told Julie, 'we're going out into the paddock and I'm going to teach you how to make Pinocchio stop and go when you want him to.'

Leaving Lewis holding the black pony, she turned away. All around her was a scene of activity. Ponies were being led out of the corral and ambulance drivers were helping to lift children up on to mounts already saddled. Liz moved towards a group of women whom she took to be the mothers of handicapped children together with helpers. She thanked them for their interest and gave one of the helpers a task of pinning a cardboard name disc to each child's shirt or sweater.

At the railing a doctor and a woman therapist were lifting a tall gangling figure on to the back of an overweight sleepy pony. Danny was clinging desperately to the pony's white mane. A spasm of sheer terror crossed his pale face. 'I'll fall!' he gasped piteously. 'Let me get down! I don't feel well!'

'Hold the reins, Danny.' Liz's voice was gentle as she placed the reins in the thin hands. His hunched shoulders and tense features betrayed his agitation. 'Just try, Danny . . . for me. You were all right before, remember? You did so well last time and I was so proud of you. We all were. Look, there's someone standing at each side to hold you steady, and I'll be leading Silver. Nothing can happen to you, Danny. You believe me, don't you? You know I wouldn't let anything hurt you!'

'*Don't leave me!*'

'I won't, not even for a minute!' If he could remain seated on the pony for a little time she felt sure he would overcome the nameless terror that had him in its grip, the fear that had for so long barred his way towards making any progress. It was a fear she realised now that was beyond all her powers to reason away. The only weapons she possessed were patience ... and love. Perhaps if she could encourage him to look on the pony as a friend rather than a terrifying hazard ... 'Look at him, Danny, he likes you.'

But the rigid figure remained motionless.

'Guess what his name is?'

There was no response beyond a quick nervous shake of the head.

'He's called Silver, and do you know why he's so fat and lazy? Because he's been put out in a paddock for years and years. The children who used to ride him went away and forgot all about him——'

'I like that!' Malcolm paused beside Liz, a halter swinging from his hand. 'Us kids couldn't help growing up, not with all that good healthy farm milk and cream and stuff! And how could you forget a piggy animal who stuck his head in at the kitchen window wanting scraps of bread whenever he caught sight of you? It's his own fault he's so disgustingly overweight.'

Liz ignored him. 'So he was given to me for the riding school and now he's feeling ever so happy because he can be with children again. (Not horrible big boys who grew into horrible big men),' she hissed towards Malcolm who showed every indication of making further comments regarding his childhood mount.

Tentatively Danny ventured to put a hand on the shaggy grey neck. 'Would he ... like me?'

'Would he? He'd be so pleased at being taken out in the paddocks for a ride, you've no idea! How would you like to be cooped up,' just in time she realised she was on dangerous ground and hurriedly changed what she had been about to say, 'in a corral all day, waiting for someone to come along and ride you? It's lucky for him that this is the day you're going to take off. Remember?'

He shrank back nervously. 'Do I *have* to?'

'Of course not, if you don't want to, but poor old Silver'll be disappointed. He's been waiting all week to get out over the paddock. I bet he could hardly wait for today to come!'

'What an exaggeration!' Malcolm hissed in her ear, his gaze on the sturdy plump pony, half-asleep in the hot morning sunshine. But who could guess at a pony's deep-down wishes, anyway?

Danny too was gazing at his mount, and for a moment surprise overcame fear as he peered down at the pony's muzzle. 'Look, he's got a sore nose. It's all red!'

Liz followed the boy's gaze. 'Oh, that? I meant to do something about it this morning, but in all the rush I forgot——'

'What's wrong with him?'

Liz laughed. 'You'd never believe it—he's sunburned! White horses get their muzzles burned sometimes.'

'*Sunburn?*' The pale face expressed only interest and concern. 'Does it hurt?'

'A little. Tell you what, I'll go and get something to put on it from the medicine box.' She turned away and hurrying to the shed, found a jar of coconut oil. When she got back to the grey pony Danny was eyeing her excitedly. 'Can I put it on? *Please*, Miss Kennedy?'

'Why not?' She handed the jar up to him and he leaned forward. The thin fingers, awkward and slow, smeared oil on the pony's pink muzzle.

'He didn't mind! He let me put it on the sore place!'

'Why should he mind? He knows you're his friend, his mate.'

'That's right.' The boy's beaming smile tore at Liz's

heart. 'We're mates, aren't we? Can I take him out now? Me and Silver, we're going out to the paddock.'

Trying not to show her surprise, Liz called to two of the helpers and together they set off, the older women clinging each side of the safety-belt handle, while Liz took the lead rope. Although Danny stiffened as he moved over the grass, the weak back muscles relaxed almost immediately and it was clear that his thoughts were still on his mount. 'He feels better now, doesn't he?'

Ahead of them Liz could see Julie, her blonde curls bobbing in the sunshine, with Lewis walking on one side of her and a woman therapist on the other, while Malcolm led the black pony.

She threw a swift backward glance towards the children awaiting their turn on the ponies. Excited voices and snatches of laughter reached her. Taiere, the small Maori boy, was playing with the white kid while the black cat and kittens were being fondled by other children seated in wheelchairs. Stan's black and white terrier, excited at finding himself such a centre of attention, barked wildly among the group.

The cavalcade moved on over the long grass, skirting overhanging branches of trees that could mean such a dangerous hazard to an unsteady rider. Presently Liz halted the riders, giving them a brief period of instruction on the control of the ponies. Danny alone sat quiet and unresponsive, but she made no attempt to force him to take part in the exercise. Already he had made progress enough for one day.

A little later, as she was helping a second section of riders to mount, Liz caught sight of the young cameraman who had visited the riding centre a week previously in order to make a commercial. Heavens, until this moment she had all but forgotten the TV team, who were to come here today for the purpose of recording a programme featuring her venture with the disabled children. As she hurried towards the tall young man she realised that a well-built fair girl standing at his side was one of the television team.

'Miss Kennedy, this is Ann——'

'Don't worry about us just now.' The smiling young interviewer turned friendly blue eyes towards Liz. 'We can see you're right in the thick of things, and that's how we like it, being where the action is! Mark's getting some good on-the-spot pictures of the ponies and riders and I can pick up the main points of the scheme later when you're through with the children. This seems to be their day. Okay?'

'Nice of you.' Liz's smile included both members of the team. 'If you wouldn't mind waiting until this lot take their turn? The children have their lunch then before they're taken back to town, and I'll be free to tell you all about it.'

The young cameraman smiled, 'Of course. Ann and I'll get busy on some notes and shots of the ponies.'

A short while later children were helped down from their mounts and helpers carried them to the rough forms that Malcolm had set up in the barn. While he and Stan attended to the ponies, Liz was kept busy filling glasses with fruit cordial and passing them around to the children seated at the long trestle tables. Already they were opening lunch boxes and enjoying the sandwiches they had brought with them.

At last everyone appeared to be catered for and Liz brought beakers of coffee to the cameraman and the girl reporter. The fair girl took it thankfully. 'That was delicious,' she said a few moments later. 'Now,' she took a notebook from the bag slung over her shoulder and poised her ballpoint, 'if you could fill me in on a few details. I think I've got most of it right.' Eagerly Liz told her of the aims of the riding school and soon the story was captured in squiggles and loops that later would feature as a news item during a programme entitled 'This Day'.

'Thanks very much, Miss Kennedy,' she put away her notebook. 'Now we're off back to town. Looks as though everyone here is too.' For lunches were being packed away and children carried into waiting cars and ambulances.

'Oh, by the way,' the cameraman said to Liz, 'the sponsors are delighted with their commercial for "To-

134

day's Girl". They said it was the girl who made the whole thing come alive. We're pretty proud of it ourselves,' he grinned. 'You'll be seeing it for yourself at the beginning of the month, and you'll get a cheque in the mail before that. Just thought you'd like to know how you made out. 'Bye for now, Miss Kennedy!'

'Goodbye, and thanks.' The fair girl threw a smile over her shoulder as she turned away.

'Quite a success, Liz, that commercial of yours!' She hadn't realised that Lewis was at her side, quiet and unobtrusive as ever.

She nodded carelessly. 'Just as well, seeing it will probably be my one and only appearance on TV. Anyway, it was as much Red's picture as mine. It's today that really mattered, though. It *was* a success, wasn't it, Lewis?'

He nodded gravely. 'Absolutely. I'd say you're really going to make out on this idea of yours, Liz. And the rest of us are with you all the way. With the publicity you'll be getting soon——'

'Thanks to you——'

'My pleasure, Liz.' He stooped to pick up Julie from her wheelchair and stood with her in his arms. 'When can I see you again?'

'I don't know. Next lesson, I guess.' Her attention was fixed on the children being settled in a waiting ambulance.

'Far too long. I'll ring you before then. Maybe come out one night to see how things are going.'

Liz was scarcely listening. 'Goodbye, Julie! See you next week!'

The child pouted. 'I wish *you* were my mother, then I could stay with you all the time——' The blue eyes danced with excitement. She plucked at her father's sleeve. 'Ask her, Daddy! Ask her if she will!'

'Don't be so silly, Julie!' Liz said lightly. But the child was not to be put off.

'*Why* can't you, Miss Kennedy?'

'Why—well, because ...' Liz wished Lewis would come to her aid, but instead the silence deepened.

Over the curly blonde head he was eyeing her with a

135

glance she failed to interpret. To cover her sudden feeling of confusion she said quickly, 'Next week, then,' and moved away to help Taiere from his wheel-chair. Soon crutches and wheelchairs were whisked away, vehicles moved up the drive and as suddenly as they had come, the procession vanished.

In the barn Evelyn was gathering up glasses. Liz helped her and afterwards went outside to Malcolm, who was sorting bridles and gear into piles belonging to separate ponies. He looked up with a grin. 'Happy about today, Liz?'

She bent to help him. 'Am I ever? If you only knew how many times I've pictured it all happening, and then to find it all really coming true——'

'Funny how only one father seems to come out here with the kids,' Malcolm murmured thoughtfully, as he untangled a stirrup leather from its mate.

'You mean Lewis Ridgway? Oh well, I guess Julie's all he's got. What with having lost his wife years ago and Julie being——'

'Tough luck. But this Lewis guy, he seems pretty interested in what goes on here at the riding centre. He's got swags of dough. Could finance the whole show if he were keen enough——' He broke off, for obviously Liz wasn't listening. 'Penny for them?'

'Oh, I was just thinking about Danny. Did you notice how different he was today? He actually wanted to go over the paddock on Silver——'

Malcolm's dark eyes glimmered with a teasing light. 'Thanks to your cruel slander. Mean to horses, she said. Forgetful . . . animal-hater!'

Liz laughed and helped him to untangle a halter rope. She had already forgotten Malcolm. She was wondering how long it would be before she would see Peter again. She was longing to tell him of her success and how the children had reacted to their first riding lesson. After all—her busy fingers paused and she stared unseeingly out over the fenced paddocks—even a man who happened to be in love with someone else could be interested in her project. And he *was* interested, she was certain of it!

Almost as though he had tuned in on her wave-length, at that moment the telephone shrilled in the barn and hurrying back to pick up the receiver, she caught the well-remembered tones. 'That you, Liz? How did things go today?'

'Tremendous! I just couldn't tell you——'

'You could, you know! Tomorrow. I've just had a ring from a bloke I know. He's got a job as ranger over in the State Forest. Those pine plantations are a great place for a ride—I thought you might like to come along with me. It's a fair distance, but we could truck the horses out there. Don't forget to bring your swim-ming togs ... we could take the horses for a swim in the tide on the way back. What do you say, Liz?'

'Oh, I'd love that!' When would she ever learn to curb her natural enthusiasm? The way she sounded, he'd think ... he'd think ...

'What time shall I be ready?'

'We'll make an early start. Nine too early for you?'

'No, it'll be fine.' It's never too early to see *you*, her heart was saying.

'See you, then. 'Bye.'

Why was it, she wondered, replacing the receiver in its cradle, that just the sound of his voice could make life all at once so different? Exciting, unexpected, wonderful!

The feeling was still with her when she awoke on the following morning. Absurd, this happiness that was flooding her simply because Peter was taking her riding in the pine plantations today. Deep down a small voice warned her that such happiness couldn't last. She thrust it away. What matter? Why not enjoy the unexpected outing? He was in love with someone else, she knew, so there was no need to make a big production of it. A day away from the riding centre, a ride through the forests, it was nothing. Why then did she have this feeling of exhilaration, as though she were riding high? Riding for a fall, Liz? Once again she smothered the small niggle in her mind and went out to the paddock to find Red. How dreadful if he had chanced to cast a shoe or developed a return of an old injury to his leg, today of all days. At that moment he whinnied and came cantering towards her. Even the sight of the bridle she carried failed to curb his enthusiasm. Clearly the chestnut too welcomed an opportunity to be out and away from the fenced paddocks that had so recently become his home.

When a long grey car towing a double horse-float appeared in the drive Liz was waiting, her saddle, bridle and sheepskin rug lying in a heap on the grass, her brief black bikini rolled in a towel alongside. She had told herself that today she would think of nothing but the ride ... yet the moment she caught sight of him striding towards her her pulses fluttered and the sunshiny day, the breathless blue sky merged into a heady wave of excitement.

'Hi, Liz,' his gaze rested on the girl standing near the corral, 'it's about time you had a chance of a ride yourself.'

'I'm looking forward to it.' She led the chestnut towards the float where a big grey horse already stood. his hoofs beating an impatient tattoo on the timber floor.

'Me too.' His look was warm and intent. The pounding of hoofs increased in volume as he led the chestnut forward and fastened down the flap of the float. 'It's not every day of the week I get a chance of taking out a girl like you,' the expression in the hazel eyes conveyed more than the words, 'and one who can ride too!'

Her soaring spirits fell with a plop. Of course, Beryl was no rider. It was the single advantage she held over the other girl, if one could term such a trifling accomplishment an advantage.

'Hop in!' She slipped into the passenger seat, glancing back over her shoulder to the two horses' heads with their flowing manes, one grey, one chestnut, in the float behind.

'Goodbye! Goodbye!' Evelyn had come to the porch to see them off. 'Have a good day!'

Liz smiled and lifted a hand in farewell, then they were moving away, swinging into the quiet road that was sharply perfumed with the pungent smell of tall white daisies that raised their long stems from the fern. Unbidden, the sense of wild happiness came surging back. Was it because of the bronzed profile at her side?

'I had a word with the ranger,' he was saying, 'about riding over the tracks in the plantation. Just a matter of getting permission, but it's okay.'

'Isn't it always allowed?'

He shook a dark head. 'Not if the timber experts happen to be zooming through the plantations on that particular day. Or if it's too dry no one can get near the place on account of the fire risk. But today,' he swung around and sent a happy grin in her direction, 'everything's just fine.'

They sped past clay banks cut into the tea-tree-covered hills around them and presently through a gap in the hills Liz caught a glimpse of the sea. Intensely blue, violet-shadowed, with breakers rolling in on an expanse of black sand. Then they were taking a twisting track that led upwards towards a fringe of tree-ferns silhouetted against the skyline. She realised that he was driving with care, avoiding potholes and rough patches, making the journey as smooth as possible for the horses in the swaying float behind them. On and on ... now they were swinging down a steep slope edged with fern and tightly-curled fronds of lacy pungas. It seemed to Liz that there was nothing in the world but the endless range of hills, tea-tree-covered, the dark green bushes starred with their myriad tiny white blossoms.

'How'd things go yesterday with the kids?' he asked suddenly.

So he had remembered about the riding lesson. 'Oh, it was a real success! You've no idea! I just wished you could have been there to see it all——' She checked herself, aghast. There she went again! She might just as well be saying: 'I love you. I want you ... all the time. Without you, nothing is worth while.'

'I will be—next time!'

'The ponies,' she said faintly, making an effort to choose her words with more care, 'the ones we got at the sale—they all behaved perfectly. Stood as still as could be while the children got mounted, just as if they knew what it was all about.'

He nodded, his eyes on a curve of road ahead. 'They looked a quiet bunch.'

'And the most marvellous thing happened! One child, a boy called Danny . . . he's most dreadfully nervous. Frightened of just about everything, and especially horses. But today he forgot all about being scared, and I'm hoping that next time——'

'Rewarding, eh?'

'That's not the word for it! It would be just fantastic to have every single one of them relaxed and happy on the ponies! With Danny it would mean a lot more than just getting over his fear of riding. It would lead on to his acceptance of other things as well, things he's simply terrified of now, like learning to use crutches——'

He nodded. 'I get it. How about the others?'

'Oh, they were so happy! Just to see their faces! Young Julie, she sat upon Pinocchio just as though she'd been there on his back a dozen times. We had such a lot of helpers turn up too—I couldn't believe it. And then——'

'How about Ridgway?' he cut in. 'Did he turn up?' There was a note of urgency in his tone that puzzled her.

'Lewis? Oh yes, he's planning to come out for every lesson. He seems to have the time to spare, and of course he thinks the world of Julie. It must be dreadful for her—I mean, to have no mother as well as being born a spastic. Yet she's the brightest, happiest child I've ever met. Malcolm's a terrific help,' she ran on. 'He comes over almost every day. I'm going to miss him a lot when he starts 'varsity in town next year.'

He didn't appear to be listening. 'Lewis comes out every week?'

'Why yes.' She wondered again at his interest in a man he scarcely knew. 'He's got a fast car and the inclination.'

'That's right.'

She couldn't fathom him in this odd satirical mood. To change the subject she said brightly, 'And what do you think? The TV camera team turned up too, so that means there should be some good publicity pretty soon. It might even bring in some funds to help along with all the things we need. New equipment, a decent concrete ramp—oh, oodles of improvements.'

'Lewis again?' He threw her a swift look, raised black brows.

She nodded. 'He offered to help out in that line. Seems he has a lot to do with advertising in his work, and of course having Julie at the riding school, he's interested——'

'Oh, he's interested all right. I've noticed.'

Liz, darting a glance towards the closed face, was nonplussed. She couldn't understand him in this strange mocking mood.

'He's certainly a man of ideas, I'll give you that!' His tone was quietly controlled. 'I take it that "Today's Girl" was his idea too?'

'Yes ... it was.' There seemed no pleasing him in this sudden dark humour. 'I thought,' she ventured in the growing silence, 'that when it's such a help towards the funds and everything, you'd be ... pleased.'

'*Pleased?* About having Ridgway hanging around all the time, shoving his oar into things?' Liz found herself regretting ever having introduced Lewis's name into the conversation, though for the life of her she could see no reason for his annoyance. If such a thought hadn't been so utterly fantastic, if things had been different between them, she might almost have imagined him to be filled with unreasoning jealousy. Yet he hadn't objected to Malcolm's helping her at the centre. She simply couldn't make him out. She decided to ignore his odd attitude.

'McGinty,' she said, 'is a pet. He was a great success when the children came yesterday. I don't think any of them had ever been able to handle a kid before. And did he enjoy all the attention! He was the star of the show, believe me!'

'Good.'

Determinedly she struggled on. She'd make him lose that dark abstracted look that had come with the mention of Lewis's name. Poor Lewis, who was only trying to help her after all. Anyone would think, looking at Peter's glowering expression, that he was in love with her himself. Anyone who didn't know him, that was.

'Darryl came for a riding lesson when the children had left.'

'He did?' At last she appeared to have captured his attention. The stern features relaxed a little.

'I'm afraid he wasn't too happy about being forced to ride a shaggy little pony. Seems his ideas run more to racehorses and flighty thoroughbreds.'

'But you made him take the pony?'

She laughed. 'I had to. He knows nothing about riding, not a thing! I don't believe he's ever been up in the saddle before!'

'He didn't try to put one over you? Take off up the road and away?'

'He didn't have much chance! Cobber always comes to a dead halt when he gets as far as the front gate. If I'd allowed him to take Red as he wanted to, goodness knows what would have happened! He tells me he's coming back for more lessons, so I suppose it will be a battle with him every time!'

She wondered at his interest in the boy's riding progress. Was he planning to change matters when he became Darryl's stepfather? After he and Beryl—— Oh, why did she keep forgetting about Beryl? She sighed and glanced ahead to the hills, clothed in dense pine trees, their outlines sharp and spiky against the intense blue bowl of the sky.

Like the sombre forests of an old German fairytale, row after row of dark green pines stretched away into the distance, broken by long corridors of firebreaks. Soon they were swinging in at the entrance to the vast plantations where the air was spiced with the clean sharp tang of the pines and the wind sighed overhead with the sound of distant surf.

'We'll leave the float here and take the horses.' Peter was pulling in close to the nearest line of trees and soon he was leading both horses out on to the grass.

Liz gazed up at the powerful grey. 'He's a big fellow. What do you call him?'

'He's Troy. Reliable type. Takes a bit of handling, but he's got a good action. Hold him for me, will you, Liz, while I saddle Red?'

'Troy.' Lightly she stroked the big grey muzzle. 'I like that name. It's perfect for a big fellow like this. He'd be,' thoughtfully she studied the muscular frame, 'how old?'

'I reared him from a foal ten years ago. Don't take any notice of him,' he added, for the massive head was moving from side to side, 'you can't believe a word he says!'

Liz laughed. He helped her to mount, then swung himself up on Troy. She couldn't help but think how well the big grey suited the man who sat him with such careless ease. She would like to have snapped a picture of Peter on Troy against a background of this undulating sea of pines. She had brought her Instamatic with her, but how could she snap a picture without having him gain an entirely false impression. He'd think... What would he think? That she was fast becoming to care for him, quite a lot. That try as she would she couldn't seem to wrench her gaze from his strong features.

Presently both horses were flying at a gallop down the long grassy lane of a firebreak. Liz leaned forward, urging Red on, and soon their mounts were racing neck and neck. At length Peter pulled his horse to a walk and Red fell in beside Troy. Long dark hair streaming behind her ears, face flushed, Liz was enjoying every moment of the ride.

After a time they turned off into a narrow path winding among a plantation of young pines. Now they were forced to ride in single file and soon they came in sight of a hut deep in the green depths of the forest. The ranger, surrounded by his dogs, appeared in the doorway, a lean brown young man whose startled gaze changed to one of delight.

'Peter! You're just in time for lunch. Come on in—

143

billy's on the boil inside.'

They tethered the horses, then entered the small timber hut, austere and spotlessly clean. Soon they were seated at a table in a tiny kitchen, drinking cups of tea and helping themselves to thick slices of bread; spreading it with butter, honey or jam. The two men discussed the ever-present need for fire prevention in the pine forests through the dry summer months ahead. Liz gathered that a radio was being installed at the headquarters camp with an extension in the ranger's truck and two portables for the working gangs. The workmen were proud of their recently acquired fire engine, and soon they were getting a look-out tower to be manned by a watcher on duty through the day and night for fire danger. Liz was content to listen, and gaze towards Peter. She didn't get many opportunities of being able to gaze at him without anyone being aware of her interest. At that moment he turned towards her and hastily she picked up the thick white china cup, brought her mind back to what the ranger was saying.

'It's fairly lonely up here in the plantation, but I'm determined to stick it out for a year or two. It's the best way I know of getting some money saved up. No distractions, no outings, nothing to spend it on.' He grinned. 'Dull, but worth while. At least it is when you happen to have something worth saving for—and believe me, Lois comes right at the top of that category. I'd do a lot more than that if it meant getting a home together quicker for us.' He passed around cigarettes and leaned forward to hold a lighter towards Liz. 'Lois has had a raw deal all the way. Looked after a mob of brothers and sisters for years after her parents died, and now, just when she could be free, she's taken on caring for an ailing elderly uncle. Trust her to be there when something or someone has to be looked after and no one else in the family will take on the job! That's why I want to make it all up to her, if I can—how about you, Peter? Still single?' He grinned towards Liz. 'Can't you do something about it, Miss Kennedy?'

144

If only she could! Liz summoned up a shaky smile and tried to sound nonchalant. 'Don't look at me! I scarcely know the man!'

The ranger's appreciative glance swept over Liz, taking in her heightened colour and downcast lashes. 'What's wrong with Peter anyhow? And what the heck's time got to do with it?'

What indeed? How long had she known him? A few weeks? A lifetime? A swift glance in his direction told her nothing, for his eyes had a curiously veiled expression. Avoiding a cloud of cigarette smoke perhaps ... or an awkward question? But trust him, she thought ruefully the next moment, to have the situation well in hand. 'Liz has other ... things on her mind.'

Has she indeed? And what would you know about that? It's you, Peter, who are on my mind every day, every night, all the time! Even if I live to be a hundred, I'll never forget today, just because we're together. To you, I know, it means nothing, but that makes no difference. I know something else too. Danger flags are flying in all directions, there's nothing ahead but pain and disappointment, but that doesn't make any difference either! She turned away to crush the ash from her cigarette, fearful of betraying the secret that the ranger had all but stumbled on. What was Peter saying now? Something about handicapped children. Liz had got her idea off the ground and now she was well away. There'd be no stopping her now she'd got started. At any other time she would have been roused to instant enthusiasm over the fulfilment of her scheme. Today she had to force herself to explain to the ranger the aims and objects of the riding centre.

They chatted for a while over cigarettes, then in spite of the pleas of the lonely man in the hut to stay a little longer, they took their leave.

'Why not go and have a look through the State Forest Park that bounded the pine plantations?' the ranger suggested as he came to see them off. 'There are fifty-five thousand acres of it, with lots of native bush.'

Peter turned to Liz. 'What do you say? Like to take

a look through the bush?'

'Love to!'

'Right! We'll be on our way!' Goodbyes were said and soon they were once more galloping along an endless corridor where tall dark trees enclosed them on either side and the air was sharp and spicy with the pungent scent of pines. As the end of the firebreak came in sight they slowed the horses to a trot. Now they were in sight of the great natural giants of the bush, tawa, kauri, rewa-rewa, their leafy branches piercing the blue far overhead, while beneath low-growing ferns and bushes made a filtered shade. They found a track and moved deeper into the bush. Here the horses' hoofs made no sound against the layers of moss and dried leaves on the narrow path and the bell-like notes of a tui sounded clear on the still air.

After some time they passed two trampers, packs on their backs, and a little further on they caught the sound of something crashing through the undergrowth. Swiftly Peter put a hand on Red's bridle as both horses paused, ears pricked and eyes alert. The next moment a wild pig emerged from the bushes, to vanish among the dense undergrowth at the side of the track.

'He's safe enough.' Peter indicated a notice nailed to a tree trunk. 'No fires. No shooting.' 'See those old ruins of buildings through the trees? They're the relics of an old saw-milling industry. They used to cut a lot of kauri here in the days of the first settlers——'

'Awful thought, cutting down those forest giants!' Her gaze travelled far upwards to where the boles of giant kauri trees rose undeviating for upwards of a hundred feet. 'Some of these trees must have been growing here long before the white man ever came to New Zealand.'

'Or the Maori. They were in great demand in the early days for making spars for the sailing ships. No need to worry about their fate now, though. These big fellows in the State Forest Park are protected, and a good thing too!'

Liz pulled on her rein, listening. 'Can you hear

146

water running somewhere? Come on, let's go and see!' She urged her mount forward and together she and Steve swept over a fern-covered rise. Below them, almost concealed by thickly-growing bush, they caught the faint sheen of water. As they came nearer they caught sight of a man moving along beside the banks and further on a party of women were collecting stones from the edge of the stream.

When they reached the water Liz dropped lightly down from the saddle. It was at once clear as to the reason why 'rock-hounds' had taken the trouble to come to this remote spot, for among the shallows gleamed smooth stones shading from tones of milky-white to pink and topaz and jade. Bridles looped over their arms, they moved along the banks and Peter suddenly bent to pick up a smooth violet-coloured pebble. 'Like it?'

'Thank you. It happens to be my lucky colour.' She added, at his glance of surprise, 'I'm a February bod and I love mauve!'

'Thanks for telling me! A bit of information like that might come in useful, one of these days!' Once again he was laughing at her. Liz fingered the cool stone that was so pleasant to the touch.

They followed the stream around the next bend where they came in sight of another party of trampers. Then once again they got on their mounts. As they rode on over the track she sniffed the air appreciatively. 'Funny—I keep getting drifts of the most heavenly perfume, yet I can't think what it could be!' She was glancing around her towards the tangled tree-ferns, clustered green five-finger and tall spears of flax. Nothing there to produce the delightful scent.

'It's the flowers of the cabbage tree,' Peter told her. 'Sometimes it drifts for miles on the breeze and once you've caught it, it's unforgettable.'

Liz thought that today everything was unforgettable. Just being alone with him, the sight of the strong bronzed face, the hazel eyes with their swiftly changing expressions. It all added up to a feeling of completeness, of happiness and content.

They were progressing now at a walking pace, for the track twisted among thorny climbers and often their way was barred by long ropes of trailing supplejack. At other times the horses were forced to pick their way over stringy black punga logs lying across the path, or the leafy branches of a tall forest giant that had come crashing to the ground during a winter storm.

He pulled on the reins. 'Let's turn back, shall we?'

She felt she could have gone on for ever under the sun-burnished sky, with the green bush all around them, and Peter ... It all came back to him. Surprisingly she realised now that the sun was lower in the sky than she had noticed. She sighed. 'Okay.' There was still the ride back to the pine plantations, she comforted herself.

But it was over all too soon and a little later she found herself seated once more in the car waiting at the edge of the line of trees. Then she remembered that they planned to swim the horses in the surf on the way back and she felt happier.

It seemed such a little time before they came in sight of the white-flecked sea and presently they left the car at the top of the cliff. Once again in the saddle, Liz guided Red down a winding path where loose rubble and small stones dislodged by the horses' hoofs went tumbling down the steep slopes. When they dropped down on to the beach, breakers were pounding in on a limitless expanse of black sand. Liz took her bikini from her saddlebag. 'Be with you in a minute!' On the shore, thickly edged with tall, densely-growing flax, she changed swiftly, but when she ran down the sand, the saddles were lying in a heap and Peter was waiting for her, lean and brown and muscular in swimming trunks. His hand was placed beneath her foot and she had sprung up on to the back of the chestnut. She pressed his side with her heel and both horses moved over the wet sand and plunged into a shower of spray.

Once over the line of breakers the horses swam out into the deep, only their heads visible as they moved out with the tide. Liz, clinging with her knees to the wet sides of her mount, her hair drenched and face beaded with drops of sea-water, sent a laughing glance back over her shoulder.

'Now!' Peter called, as an oncoming white-crested comber came surging towards them. They turned and the next second horses and riders were swept inshore on the force of the wave. Liz felt a delightful sense of exhilaration in the surge of the sea, the relaxing yet invigorating force of the breakers. It was sheer joy to search for Peter's dark head amidst a shower of spray, before they both turned and once again urged their mounts towards an expanse of glittering sea.

At last the horses scrambled out on to the sand at a point a distance along the shore from where they had entered the water. Soon Liz and Peter were urging their mounts to a canter as they moved along the tide-line, the flying hoofs leaving indentations in the wet sand behind them. When they reached the saddles, Liz dismounted. Cool and refreshed, conscious of a delicious sense of relaxation engendered by sun and sea, she flung back her wet hair and gazed around her. Against a backdrop of sun-flecked sea, a mirage danced over the dazzling ironsands, pricked with a thousand diamonds in the afternoon sunlight. All at once she met his glance and felt her heart contract. How vibrantly alive he looked! The sort of man who would look after a girl. What would it be like to be loved by such a man? With an effort of will she turned away and picking up her towel began to dry her hair, but all the time the crazy thoughts went spinning through her mind. If she didn't look directly towards him he mightn't suspect ... that she was in love. Love! Once before she had imagined herself to be in love, but how could she know the difference until she had met a man like Peter? I'm in love with him, she marvelled, just like that! I have been ever since that first day we met here at the beach.

'Hey, Liz , you're miles away!' He had flung himself down on the hot sand and leaning on an elbow, gazing up at her, laughter glimmering in his eyes. 'Come back! No, come on down here with me!' A swift tug at her hand and he had pulled her down on the sand at his side. 'You looked awfully sad all of a sudden. Come on now, what's wrong?'

The intent glance that so often seemed to probe her innermost thoughts raked her face. She picked up a handful of sand, watched it sift through her fingers. Like time, she thought, like days with him, running out. 'That first day, on the beach,' she murmured inconsequently, 'you had on an orange-coloured shirt——'

He was grinning. '*Had* is right!'

'I know. It was all my fault. I'll get you another one when I go to town next time, to make up.'

He didn't answer. Very gently he put a hand against her hot cheek and she didn't know whether it was the dazzle of the sun or the dazzle in her heart that was sending waves of excitement through her. She only knew that if he kissed her again, she'd forget everything else, even Beryl. Being with him was like being under a spell, nothing else mattered. Surely she could snatch one day from fate, enjoy the deep enchantment of being in love. There would be so many days in the future when she would be far away from him, a whole lifetime of them! Sun, sea and the salty relaxation of the surf all conspired against her and as he drew her close she was swept by an aching longing to feel his lips on her own.

When he released her she was still caught in the poignant happiness of his kiss and for a moment she failed to realise that they were no longer alone on the beach.

'I could swim further out in the surf than either of you!' The moment of magic splintered into fragments as, startled, she glanced up into Darryl's small sulky face. He was standing facing them, hands thrust into the pocket of his jeans.

'You reckon?' Peter lay back on the sand, hands crossed behind his head. His glance slid to a car standing on the grass beneath spreading pohutukawa trees not far distant. 'Where did you spring from anyway? Did your mum bring you down here?'

'I don't need *her*! I can drive! Didn't you know? I can ride a horse too,' the light bragging tones went on.

'It wouldn't matter to me how high-spirited or wild it was!' He swung an accusing face towards Liz. 'If only you'd give me something to ride, Miss Kennedy, instead of a corny old pony, I'd show you what I could do. I bet I could go out a lot further in the surf than either of you! No trouble!'

'I wouldn't advise it, mate,' Peter's voice was crisp. 'Beryl know you're taking the car out by yourself?'

'She knows.' Darryl gave a childish grin, half fearful, half swaggering. He kicked at the shells lying on scintillating sand. 'Well, anyhow, she will soon when I get back.' His bravado faltered in the face of the man's direct look. 'She's not *my* mother,' he muttered half under his breath.

'Near enough.'

For answer the boy pulled a face. Then, turning, he made his way over the sand, wading through the clear stream on the way back to the grassy patch beneath the trees. When he reached the car he got inside, slammed the door and started the motor. A moment or two later he went hurtling up the road, to be lost to sight around a bend of the track winding up the steep bush-clad hill.

Peter's mouth was grim. 'He needs a man around the place to straighten him up a bit! The way he's going it looks like his mother's heading for a whole heap of trouble one of these days!'

'I guess you're right.' But to herself Liz was saying, Did Beryl too need a man, one man in particular, whom she had never ceased to love, in spite of an earlier marriage, followed by a new life in another country? 'Perhaps,' she said in a thick, unnatural voice, 'he'll be getting one . . . before long.'

He threw her a swift surprised glance. 'Now just how did you drop on to that? It's supposed to be a dead secret. You don't miss much, do you, Liz? You must be well up in the subject of love to catch on so quickly.' He grinned and made to take her hand, but swiftly she moved away.

'Not really.' The bitter pain that was flooding her made normal speech difficult. Could that be her own voice, so low and charged with emotion? Springing to her feet, she turned aside to hide her trembling lips. 'I'm off to get changed.' Picking up her bundle of clothing, she stumbled blindly away over the sand.

So it was true, the suspicion she'd had all along that he was merely filling in time with her. Only a stupid nit like herself would have read anything more into his friendship. Her idea of providing a riding school for the handicapped had intrigued him, just as she herself had amused him, for a time. But it was Beryl who was his real life. The pain in her heart was as sharp as a physical wound. Once he had told her lightly, teasingly, *prophetically* as things had turned out, 'When I find my own special kind of girl, you'll be the first to know!'

Behind the thick wall of densely growing flax bushes she paused and with unsteady fingers slipped from her bikini. It was easier to bear the pain now she was out of range of the disturbing masculine magnetism that seemed so hard to combat. The shaking of her hands made her movements slow and awkward, but at last she was ready. She ran a comb through damp, wind-blown hair, rolled her bikini in the towel. Well, she'd have to face him some time. Her lips were still a little out of control and there was a stinging moisture behind her eyes, but she supposed that to everyone else (and why not admit that by 'everyone' she meant one man who she happened to love?) she would appear to be perfectly normal. Heartbreak need not show if you were careful to avoid looking directly into perceptive hazel eyes. And anyway, she reflected as she pushed through flax spears and made her way over the sun-flecked ironsands, the day was almost at an end. Her last day alone with Peter, for after this she would make certain not to run the risk of putting herself in this dangerous, heartbreaking position. She slowed her steps, reluctant to face him, afraid that he would guess how deeply she cared. She was such a fool at conceal-ing her emotions, especially where he was concerned! All this time at the back of her mind there had been a crazy hope that somehow a miracle would happen.

Well, now she knew. There wasn't the slightest chance in the wide world of his ever returning the feeling she had for him. But she couldn't dawdle along the sand for ever, and when at last her dragging footsteps brought her back to him she told herself that after all she need not have worried. For he looked relaxed and cheerful. He had changed back into shirt and shorts, his dark hair springing back in damp waves from a bronzed forehead.

'You should have told me.'

Her heart flipped. 'Told you?' Why was he regarding her in that speculative, concerned manner? Her glance was evasive.

'You've gone all white under that brand-new tan of yours! Stayed in the water a bit long, by the look of things. I'd better make up for it by getting you home right away!' To her relief he began to saddle the horses.

He brought Red to her side and she placed a bare brown foot on the strong tanned hand he extended and leaped up into the saddle. For a moment he stood motionless, smiling up at her. Just as though, she thought wildly, there were nothing to keep them apart ... no Beryl. 'I forget sometimes that a girl might not be used to being in the surf for hours at a time. Not like me, in training all the year round with the surf club. I won't let it happen again, Liz.'

Her smile was tremulous. 'Not your fault,' she said huskily. No, the fault lay with herself and her own stupid vulnerable heart. For her own sake she knew there would never be a next time. That way danger lay.

CHAPTER 8

TORN by her inner conflicts, in the following week Liz threw herself more than ever into her duties. Once she had imagined that to realise her dream of helping the handicapped would be to gain for herself perfect contentment; that it would be all she would ever ask of life. But that was before she had met Peter, and things hadn't worked out that way. Not that she wasn't pleased with her progress with the riding centre. The work itself was deeply satisfying, so far as it went. If only there wasn't always the dreary hopeless longing to see Peter again. The sense of desolation, the despair that swept over her at moments when her guard was down, all pin-pointed what life could have meant, with him. How could she have known that outside love's magic circle, even success in one's chosen field failed to satisfy? That nothing could take the place of being loved by the one man in the world to whom you had been foolish enough to have lost your heart?

She supposed she should feel grateful for interests that demanded all her time and attention, she told herself forlornly when the telephone rang for the sixth time since breakfast. The speaker was a woman, a reader of one of the magazines that had recently featured an article dealing with the riding centre at Rangiwahia. Liz thanked the enquirer for her offered donation and told her yes, they were always glad of extra helpers on the weekly visits of the handicapped children. Liz would add the newcomer's name to the roster of helpers. She went on to detail the route by motorway from the city to the riding school. It was a pattern to which she was fast becoming accustomed, for the recent publicity afforded to her venture by magazines and newspaper articles had sparked an im-

154

mediate interest in a sympathetic public.

She had been pleasantly surprised too at the response to the TV feature with its pictures of children riding their ponies, together with interviews with medical superintendents and therapists. Screened at news time on an early evening session, the feature had captured viewers' imagination and from that night onwards donations, offers of help and gifts of ponies and gear had continued to pour in. It seemed she had actually launched her venture successfully at last and from now on things should run fairly smoothly. She should be so happy, and yet . . .

Even her sister Helen had written that for once in her life she had to admit to being proved in the wrong. Liz's crazy scheme looked like turning into something worthwhile after all. Although, Helen had pointed out with sisterly candour, she couldn't help thinking that in spite of the rewarding nature of Liz's work, when you came right down to it there was really nothing to match marriage with the right man. Had Liz met up with any eligible young farmers yet? There must surely be one or two stashed away up there in the bush!

One was sufficient, Liz reflected bleakly, when the man in question happened to be Peter! She drew in a short sharp breath. There she went again, thinking of *him*! In a spurt of anger she tore the letter into fragments, scattering the pieces into the waste paper basket beneath the desk.

The fact that Danny was at last making definite progress was the one gleam of light in the darkness of spirit that caused her to sleep fitfully and to pick listlessly at Evelyn's wholesome, well-cooked meals. Danny was now much more relaxed and when she was with him Liz forgot, for a little time, her own heartache. No longer did he flinch and hold back nervously on being lifted up on to Silver's broad back. What she had scarcely dared to hope for had happened. His newly-found affection towards the shaggy white pony had pushed fear into the background of his mind. On the last riding day he had even responded to instruction, and his pride and excitement as the weak hands pulled on the rein and turned the pony in another direction was to Liz well worth all her patient weeks of gentle perseverance. If only she could tell Peter of her victory with Danny. The traitorous thought sneaked into her mind and was as swiftly thrust aside.

Peter. The only way in which she could carry on with her life here was to try to make her mind a blank. But how to do that when you froze to instant awareness at each peal of the telephone, and your thoughts flew into a turmoil at the mere appearance of a long grey car in the driveway? Or the sight of a tall masculine figure approaching the cottage? A figure that might be him, only of course it never was!

She knew that he had been away for a week, buying sheep in the South Island, but he would soon be returning to Arundel and then ... If he should contact her once again somehow she would have to steel herself, make him understand she had no intention of seeing him again—ever. It was possible to continue with her life as usual, almost, but if she came face to face with him even for a minute she had a frightening suspicion that all her good resolutions would vanish like manuka smoke in the wind and she would be at the mercy of her own vulnerable heart and his mocking smile.

Once again the telephone shrilled through the big room and abstractedly she lifted the receiver.

'Peter here.'

'Peter!' Her heart gave a great leap, then just in time she remembered what she had schooled herself to do. If only he didn't make it too difficult.

'Just thought I'd check up,' came the deep, friendly, *heart-catching* tones. 'I've been away for a while, down south. Had you noticed?'

Had she noticed! 'Yes, no—I mean I heard——'

'You're stalling, Liz, but I'll forgive you if you let me take you out tonight!' He sounded as confident as ever. 'Seeing you on TV isn't the same, Liz, but it was something! That programme on the riding school was darn good viewing, let everyone in to what's going on up here at Rangiwahia. Happy with it?'

'Oh yes, I was!' Nervousness made her add: 'Did you happen to see the commercial too?'

'It was tremendous! Great of you, and old Red gave a good account of himself! You know something, Liz?' She caught the teasing note in his voice. 'You'll be famous around the place pretty soon. Everyone'll know Today's Girl with the old-fashioned sweetness in her smile!' As usual, she thought with a pang, he was laughing at her. 'I thought we'd celebrate your success?'

'Celebrate?'

'Why not? It doesn't take long to zip into town and I've booked a table for two at the Matador. What do you say?'

The temptation to go with him was so strong she had to force the longing aside. She mustn't give in to herself. 'I'm sorry,' she hoped he would lay the blame on the connection for the unevenness of her husky tones, 'but I'm afraid I can't make it tonight. Some of the heads of the hospital in town are making a special trip up here to see me—at least, I think they are——'

'Tomorrow night, then?'

'No, no——'

'More conferences?' How gay and confident he sounded, just as though there was nothing to keep them apart. Why not, he already had Beryl and marriage plans in mind. Who was to know if once in a while he took out another girl for a night's entertainment in the city?

'The same ones,' she managed breathlessly. 'You see, I'm not quite sure which night they're coming and I have to be here, just in case.'

'How about next week, then?'

'I'm sorry——' If only he wasn't making it so difficult, and it didn't hurt so much to say the words.

'*You're* sorry! Well, tough luck!' She caught an odd inflection in his tone ... bewilderment, surprise, disappointment? 'But we'll make it one of these days. Some other time, then. Be seeing you, Liz.'

''Bye, Peter.' The words lingered in her mind like

the tolling of a distant bell. Goodbye. Goodbye. He wasn't the type of man to plead with her to change her mind. There'd be no need to spell it out. It was her own wayward heart that was proving so difficult to discipline. Yet somehow, no matter how painful, she must cut the ties that over the past few weeks had strengthened to ever-tightening bonds, at least so far as she was concerned. Short of flight, and circumstances put that out of the question, this was the only way. Let him think what he pleased of her seemingly puzzling behaviour.

Nor did her decision grow any easier to maintain as the slow days crept by and there was no further word from him. But life went on and outwardly everything proceeded much as usual. One morning the mail brought yet another generous cheque from the un-known donor, whom Liz still thought of as 'Mr. X', for the benefit of the riding school. Now she could at last afford to have the drive from the gate to the cottage concreted, an urgent need. Her first impulse was to rush to the telephone. She must tell Peter of her good fortune! Then she remembered, and the pain came back.

Tuesdays were the best days when, involved with the children and ponies, her own conflicts slipped into the background and the pain eased, for a time. Malcolm had fallen into a habit of coming to the cottage almost daily and was at hand to help with the ponies and the endless tasks concerned with their care. In the even-ings and at weekends Lewis had become a frequent visitor. Tonight he had brought account books with him. As he sat opposite Liz at the desk in the barn, the hanging electric light bulb illuminated his bent head and carefully tended black hair. As he opened the lined pages of a cash book Liz sighed and made a face. 'Must we?'

He smiled across at her. 'This won't take long, and it's important to know how you're going along. But if you'd rather leave it until another night, just say the word——'

'No, no. I've got everything ready for you. Here are

the cheques and this pile is all the cash donations. Receipts are on the file, and I've kept all the accounts together for payment.' As he totalled up the money, Liz found herself thinking what a good friend Lewis had proved himself to be. All this book-keeping ... it was a chore as well as something of which she had very little knowledge. Now she came to consider the matter, she really owed a lot of the success of her venture to Lewis's business acumen and expert assistance. He was friendly, yet always so correct. She could have smiled to think how ridiculous was Peter's obvious jealousy on Lewis's account. But she mustn't think of Peter.

They worked steadily for an hour, then they were interrupted by a telephone ring. Liz picked up the receiver. 'Yes?'

'Oh, Liz, this is Beryl.' The other girl seemed so excited and happy that for once she had forgotten to treat Liz with her usual brand of condescension and disdain. 'Is Peter there with you by any chance? He said something about calling around to see you about something——'

'No.'

'Well, listen, if he does come, tell him to hurry back here, will you? I've got some important news to give him. You can let him know that I've made the big decision at last!'

'I'll tell him if he comes.' Funny how perfectly ordinary she sounded, as though it was all nothing whatever to do with her, which was indeed the truth. All at once the import of the message struck her. Peter! Coming here tonight! That she couldn't endure.

Thoughtfully she replaced the receiver in its cradle. A momentous decision made between a man and a woman who were on the verge of starting a new life together? Maybe they had quarrelled and Beryl wanted to put things right between them without further delay. Or more likely the other girl had set a date on which to announce the engagement. Perhaps even a wedding day, for what need was there to wait? No wonder Beryl had sounded so happy!

'What's wrong, Liz?' She became aware of Lewis,

who was eyeing her with concern.

She stared blindly back at him, unaware of her sudden pallor or of the pain shadowing her dark eyes. 'Nothing ... just a message I had to give ... someone.'

'Sure?' His tone softened. 'You can tell *me*, you know. You look as though you've taken a shock. Not bad news?'

She felt an urge towards hysterical laughter, but instead she stilled her trembling lips, said huskily, 'It was just a call ... nothing ... important.'

'I see.' He was still regarding her thoughtfully. 'Look, you're tired tonight. All this stuff,' he glanced down at the account books and papers outspread over the desk, 'it's not urgent. But something else is. Let's take a run out—that is, if you're not expecting anyone to call here tonight?'

Although the night was warm she felt a shiver pass through her. 'No, no, nothing like that!' All at once she felt she had to escape. She couldn't wait here to endure the bittersweet misery of meeting Peter again. 'A run out in the car?' the words came jerkily. 'That would suit me fine. It's one of those evenings!' Feverishly she sprang to her feet, in her haste sending a sheaf of papers fluttering to the floor. Lewis bent to pick them up and when he straightened she noted in some other part of her mind that his hands were unsteady. And something else too struck her. He was looking animated, almost ... elated. But he only said quietly, 'Come on, then, let's go, before you change your mind!'

Change her mind! If he only knew what a fever of impatience possessed her to be away from the barn as soon as possible. If Peter came here tonight she couldn't face him, she wouldn't! It seemed an age as she waited while Lewis gathered up account books and files. Her ears alerted to every sound on the driveway outside, she wanted to cry Hurry! Hurry! as with maddening precision Lewis continued to place folders in his briefcase. At last, however, he snapped the catch and they went out into the cool freshness of evening. Not until she was seated in the car did Liz's taut nerves relax a little. As Lewis thumbed the starter she leaned forward anxiously, fearful that at any moment she might catch the gleam of car headlamps shining in at the entrance.

'You're very quiet tonight.' Lewis swung through the opening and they turned into the shadowed road.

She had been peering through the window, her gaze alerted to car lights on the hill ahead, and came back to the present with a start. 'Was I? I was just think-ing——'

'Don't! Just relax, enjoy yourself for a change. Not that you can see much at the moment, but still...' He flung her a smile. 'You certainly picked a scenic spot for your riding centre when you settled for Rangi-wahia, whatever it means.'

'I know the translation from Maori,' she answered dully. 'It means "A Shimmering Sky", a sort of break-through in the clouds.'

'Sounds great.'

'Yes.' She was speaking her thoughts aloud. 'It paints a picture. Rift in a clouded sky. Things looking up——'

'Maybe for me it's a lucky omen!' She had no idea what he meant, nor did she particularly care, for at that moment a car swept around a bush-shadowed bend and as it scraped past on the narrow road she caught a fleeting glimpse of Peter's dark head. He was heading from the direction from which they had come so evidently she had made her escape only just in time! Had she recognised Lewis's car? she wondered. Not that it mattered one way or the other. It was no concern of his where she went or who she chanced to be with. She sank back in her seat.

'That's more like it,' said Lewis. 'Now tell me, where would you like to go tonight?'

'It doesn't matter.' The next moment, realising how clearly her listless tone betrayed her heaviness of spirit, she roused herself to add hastily, 'I mean, it's all the same. There's no moon—yet.'

'Right! We'll head for the coast!'

If only, she thought wildly, he didn't take the path

leading to the cliff overlooking the sea where she had gone with Peter. But already they were swinging into another track that led through dark bush. Presently they emerged in a clearing and Lewis ran the car to the end of a grassy headland where the roar of the surf was loud in their ears. Further up the coastline, a scattering of lights indicated a township and below, the headlamps picked up the dark, wind-tossed waves.

He switched off the engine, leaving only a small bulb on the dashboard alight, then swung around to face her. All at once his tone was deep, hoarse with emotion, so un-Lewis-like that she stared at him in surprise.

'You don't know how much I've wanted this!' His arm slipped around her shoulders and before she could pull away she felt his mouth on hers. Her own lips were unresponsive, utterly without feeling.

'I love you, Liz. I have right from the beginning! Oh, I told myself I'd wait until I was a bit more sure of how you felt about me, but hell, Liz, I'm not a boy any more. A man can't wait for ever, not when he's as crazy over someone as I am about you! Look,' he said softly, 'why don't you let me take care of you, for good, I mean? Now, don't say anything,' for she had opened her mouth to protest. 'I didn't mean to come right out with it for months yet. Courting's an old-fashioned word these days, I guess, but that's what I had in mind. But seeing you tonight, watching you trying to cope with problems and finances as well as giving the kids their riding lessons . . .' Softly he caressed her hair. 'We *need* each other, Liz, whether you realise it or not!' His smile was very tender and she found herself wondering why she hadn't guessed at his feelings long ago. Aloud she said the first thing that came into her mind. 'But you scarcely know me.'

'I know you well enough, Liz. And I don't think you'd find me such a bad sort of guy to get along with. No bachelor habits, no particular vices. I've only got one obsession, and that's—loving you!'

'I know, I know, Lewis. It isn't anything like that!' His tone sharpened. 'There's someone else——'

'No,' her tone was infinitely sad, 'there's no one.'

'Well,' he let out a long sigh of relief, 'that's something. I can take it from here. I know it's a bit underhand to mention it, but don't forget, there's Julie. Together we could make a decent life for the kid, a real home. Think of it that way, Liz. Oh, I know,' he went on, very low, 'that you mightn't be all that wrapped up in me, but give me time. We'll make out. Together we'd make a great team. You'll see. Just give it a chance! Marry me, Liz,' he urged, 'and we'll set up a riding centre for the whole of the country, one that'll cater for every sort of disability you can think of. If you like we'll move somewhere else, start afresh. You'll never have another financial worry——'

'Silver stirrups, Lewis?' Her sad little smile didn't reach her eyes.

'Why not? Gold-plated if you like, every single one of them! All you have to do is just say the word. For my wife, Liz, nothing is too good——'

'You're very good to me. If only——'

Swiftly he placed a finger against her lips. 'Don't say it—the "if". "When," Liz, that's the operative word. *When* you're my wife. How does that sound to you?'

She didn't answer. It was no use. She simply had no feeling for him or if she had it wasn't the sort on which one could plan a marriage. If only he wasn't so certain that he could persuade her to change her mind.

He lowered his head and as she felt the touch of his lips on her brown hand she had an odd sensation that all this was happening to someone else. Illogically, with another part of her mind, she noticed the thinning patch on the bent dark head. Poor Lewis, he had already taken so many unexpected blows from fate—a tragically brief marriage, an adored only child born a victim of cerebral palsy. Why did he have to fall in love with her when there must be so many other women he knew who would appreciate his kindness and reserved charm?

He looked up into her eyes. 'You'd never be sorry, you know. I'd love you all my life! Think, Liz, we'd have shared interests, a happy life together with enough funds to do the things you want to for the handicapped youngsters. If you like we'd go overseas, take a look over at the other side of the world, see how your set-up here compares with what's being done along the same lines overseas. Not such a bad life, would you say? I mean, what more could one ask for?'

'Just ... love.' She scarcely realised she had spoken her thoughts aloud until he caught her up sharply.

'But I love you, Liz, truly I do. I always will. You know that——'

'Yes, I know, but——'

'I could teach you to love me, Liz ... like this.' The next moment his lips were pressed to her mouth in a tender caress. And still she felt no emotion of any sort.

'Not so bad, was it?' Lewis was saying as he gently released her. But he must have guessed how she *really* felt about him, Liz thought, for without giving her time to reply he was running on, eagerly, persuasively, 'Why waste your life waiting for something that may never come along? Could be it's all an illusion. We'll have something a lot more lasting to build on. Trust me, marry me, Liz,' his voice dropped to a low, pleading note. 'You'll never regret it, I promise you.'

She hesitated. A glance at his set face made her realise that his calm exterior hid a depth of feeling. He really cared, although up to now he had kept his emotions well under control, given nothing away. She flinched from the thought of having to inflict on him the nagging heartache she herself was suffering right now; the shamemaking misery of being hopelessly, helplessly in love with no hope of one's affection ever being returned. At this moment, no doubt, the thought came unbidden, Peter and Beryl were happily arranging the details of their approaching wedding, while she ... All at once her mood of despair faded and a desperate recklessness took over. Why not consider Lewis's offer? What did she have to lose? All that she had left now, all she would ever have, were the children. If she could make life more bearable for these unfortunate ones, wouldn't that be something worthwhile? By joining her life with Lewis she would be in a position to help them all, and especially one small motherless girl whose smile tugged at her heart. In her mind a child's voice echoed with wistful longing: 'I wish *you* were my mother.'

The thoughts went rushing wildly through her mind and she nibbled a long strand of hair in indecision. It wasn't as if she didn't like him—as a person, that was. And there wasn't the slightest question of his deep affection for her. So why not make him happy too, as well as the children? The only one who wouldn't share in the general felicity, she mused with bitter anguish, was Liz Kennedy herself, but wasn't that all her own fault? Falling in love with a man to whom she meant nothing, a man who had been in love with another girl long before she had ever met him. Because he'd smiled at her, teased her, she loved him without rhyme or reason or hope or anything else. But love, it seemed, wasn't enough. It happened and there was nothing you could do about it. Or was there? All at once everything became plain, too plain. Either you went on living here, watching Peter and Beryl enjoying their new life together, or you made Lewis happy, and with him widened the scope of your chosen work, somewhere else. Why not prove to Peter that even if he regarded her as merely a girl with an unusual goal, someone else cared enough for Liz Kennedy to ask her to marry him? Yes, *that would show him*! If only she could feel some pleasure in the prospect, in place of this frozen feeling of detachment. On a note of recklessness she heard herself say, 'Maybe I'll think about it, one of these days!'

'You will? Liz, my darling, that's the best news I've had in all my life! But why wait? Tell me now!' He was so incredulously delighted that she knew a moment of misgiving.

'I've got to think it over. Give me a little time.' Wildly she searched her mind for a reasonable excuse. 'I'm putting on a Christmas party for the children next week and I'll be awfully tied up for a while, but after that——'

'I'll be waiting on the doorstep and the moment

you're finished with the kids——' He caught her close and once again his kiss registered exactly nothing with her. Was it because of Peter—but she mustn't think of him. She realised Lewis was gazing down at her, an unreadable expression in his voice. 'You'll feel differently about me one of these days!'

So her lack of response hadn't gone unnoticed. What if he guessed the truth? The thought made her say hastily, 'You're quite sure, about me?'

'Never been so sure of anything! We'll have so much to talk about ... plans and arrangements——' He broke off, said pleadingly. 'You will make it "yes"?' He carried her fingers to his lips. 'Can't you just see Julie's face light up when she hears this news!'

'No!' Alarm sharpened her tone. 'Please, Lewis,' she begged, 'don't say anything about us. There's nothing to tell—yet.'

'Okay, then.' His indulgent smile was the nearest thing to a caress. 'If you say so, but just until I bring the ring down next week. That sounds a bit off, I know, darling, not giving you a chance to choose it yourself, but it happens to be a family tradition in our family that the bride-to-be wears the heirloom ring. It was my mother's——'

'And Edith's, I expect.' She was scarcely aware of what she was saying, but the next moment she realised that Lewis had taken her idle remark as a jealous reference to his first wife.

'It's up to you, Liz,' he said eagerly. 'I'll bring it out after the Christmas "do" and you can see what you think of it. Actually it's rather a lovely thing, a big emerald square surrounded by diamonds. But if you don't care for it you don't need to have it. Just say the word and we'll take off into town and you can choose something you like better.'

'I'd like it, of course I would, if I——' She stopped short, for how to explain that she had so little interest in the matter that one precious stone was as good as another.

'It's going to be a long week,' Lewis was saying softly.

'It'll soon go——'

'Worth it if you give me the answer I want.'

He seemed not to notice her silence. 'We'll have to make some plans for a house. I'll get an architect to draw up some designs and you can see what you think of them.'

'A house?' she echoed bewilderedly.

'Why not? We could build right here by the riding school if that's what you'd like. I could run into town to the office every day from here.'

'All that way? It would mean changing your whole way of life.'

He kissed her fingers. 'That's what I'm hoping for, my sweet. If I had you, do you think I'd care about anything ... but this ...' Once again she felt his swift caress as his mouth came down on her cold unresponsive lips.

When they got back to the cottage it was late and Evelyn and Stan had long since gone to bed. But Lewis in his present mood of elation seemed reluctant to leave. His arm was thrown around her shoulders. 'With a bit of luck, soon there won't be any more goodbyes for us——'

'No.'

Tenderly he put his hands each side of her face. 'You know something? It's just about time someone started taking care of you. Lately you've been looking—I don't know, different from when you first came here. Sort of wan-looking. You're running yourself ragged over this project of yours!'

She laughed away his concern. 'Don't be silly! I told you before, I love it.'

'Don't waste it all on the kids!'

She watched him get into the car, waving as he drove away, knowing all the time that the moment he disappeared into the night he would have passed from her mind. If only she could feel the same way about Peter! All at once she wondered if she were being fair to herself or Lewis in considering this marriage. But there was still a little time left. The children's Christmas party was a whole week away and in that time anything could happen. Perhaps even ... one more miracle! Peter's vibrant tones echoed in her mind. 'Twenty-seven miracles! Isn't that rather a lot to ask of fate?' Yet here she was, praying for one more, the most impossible one of all, and with a time limit at that! She stumbled blindly to her room and fell into bed. But hour after hour sleep eluded her as the thoughts milled endlessly through her brain. Maybe if she and Lewis went away, if they moved the riding centre to another part of the country, somewhere where there would be no danger of her running into Peter, she would be able to forget, to start afresh. But a wave of longing washed over her and she knew she couldn't tear herself away, not while he remained here. Peter, Peter, you're in my blood, part of me, and somehow, somehow I've got to stop loving you!

CHAPTER 9

IT seemed to Liz now that time was rushing inexorably by. So short a time before Lewis would be here for his answer. She *must* make up her mind. A dozen times a day she told herself that the marriage would work out, of course it would. If only she could rid herself of this feeling of a cage door about to close, shutting her away from life, from happiness, *from Peter*, for ever. Putting aside her own problems, she tried to concentrate on the party she planned to give the children at the close of the next riding lesson, the last one before the intervention of the long summer school holidays. It wasn't the children's fault that she was in no mood for festivities, and they well deserved a treat, for each one had progresssed even beyond her hopes. Julie and Taiere were now able to ride without the aid of helpers and in common with other small riders, had learned to rise to the trot. In the next term they would be taught to play mounted games such as bending around poles, lifting a cap off each and dropping it back in a can. They would enjoy their games on horseback in the New Year.

New Year ... as had happened so often during the past few days she fell into a day-dream, telling herself that Lewis was kind and intelligent and dependable. He had a personal interest in the riding centre as well, and besides all that, there was Julie. Who could help falling a willing victim to that gay laughing little face, the bright smile that made one forget the useless legs, the wheelchair waiting by the railing? Oh yes, she and Lewis certainly had a lot in common. Unconsciously she sighed. If only there were love too—or was it all an illusion as he had said? If only she could persuade herself that her deep involvement with Peter didn't matter, but in her heart she knew it did matter—terribly. Even after not seeing him since their day in the pine plantations, in the face of having as good as told him that she never wished to set eyes on him again, still she found herself waiting and hoping for some word from him. But of course nothing could be more unlikely. Whatever there had been between them—and looking back there really hadn't been much to remember—it was over. It was high time she stopped herself from jumping each time the telephone pealed. Anyway—she made an effort to will away the dreary thoughts—just because she was desolate and unhappy, was that any reason why she shouldn't do her utmost to give the children an end-of-the-year celebration?

On hearing of the Christmas party, Evelyn was enthusiastic and Stan offered his help. To prove his point he disappeared soon after breakfast, returning later carrying in his arms a fresh young pine tree. He arranged it in a corner of the barn where its spicy aromatic tang filled the air.

Malcolm, strolling in at that moment, recollected that there were boxes of Yuletide decorations stowed away in an attic of his home. Evelyn produced a long length of plastic tablecloth patterned in a gay design of reindeer and Christmas angels.

Swiftly Liz's mind was running ahead, planning the programme of festivities. One thing was for sure. There must be a gift for each child among the parcels heaped beneath the Christmas tree. But where to purchase the presents? She remembered the small township to which Peter had taken her on the day of the horse sale. How long ago it all seemed now, and how happy she'd been. Would she ever again know that wild happiness that had throbbed around her that day? *Don't think, don't remember.* Concentrate on the township. There had been a general store, but the choice there would be strictly limited, and these partygoers wouldn't be ordinary children. For her small riders she wanted gifts that would be treasured, appreciated, special. She had a swift mental picture of Taiere, the small Maori boy with the outsized grin. A wide cowboy sombrero, a silver metal holster to wear at his belt, would enable him to feel more than ever a rider of the wild west such as he envisaged himself to be while high in the saddle. A small price to pay for a child's world of enjoyment!

And Julie, darling, mischievous, heart-catching Julie ... who had once said with all the candour and truth and longing of a six-year-old, 'I wish *you* were my mother!' On a sigh she reflected: I might even be able to hand you that particular wish, little one, and as an extra, how would you settle for a thin gold chain with a locket engraved in the shape of a pony? Or maybe a tiny silver locket containing a snapshot of her beloved Pinocchio?

And how about Danny, whose courage brought a mist to her eyes? Maybe a book on the training and care of ponies would please him. Thoughts of the children dispelled for a time her own sense of desolation and heartache. In the end she decided to write to Helen who, for all her maddening habit of handing out unasked-for advice, had a soft heart where children were concerned, and an eye for a bargain! In the modern city stores she would be able to find the right gifts. Perched on a corner of the desk in the barn, Liz picked up pad and ballpoint and scribbled a note to her sister, telling her of her plans for a children's Christmas party and enclosing a list of suggested purchases. In addition Liz would be glad of party favours, novelties, tinsel streamers. The important thing was for the parcel to arrive at Rangiwahia by the end of the week. Helen, practical-minded and thrifty, could be depended upon to get good value for the limited amount of money Liz had to spare and she knew she could depend on her sister to have the parcel sent in good time.

Sure enough the huge box arrived by mail van with a day to spare, and Evelyn and Liz lifted it on to the kitchen table and drew out the contents.

It was at once evident that Helen had performed her commission faithfully. She had even included odd decorations from her own store of Christmas novelties together with sheets of sparkling coloured cellophane wrapping paper and name cards. As to the gifts for the children... 'You have to hand it to Helen,' Liz murmured to Evelyn, 'she's a wizard when it comes to shopping! Just look at this!' She snapped open a small silver locket suspended from a slender chain. 'I can put Pinocchio's picture in here. I'll cut it out from one of the snapshots Lewis gave me, and fit it in for her.'

Evelyn, busily counting Christmas crackers included in the parcel, nodded. 'It'll be the first time in his life that old pony's been in on such a fuss! But I guess Julie would rather have a picture of him than anything else you could give her.'

Liz thought she couldn't have chosen better had she herself been able to purchase the gifts. Taiere's cowboy sombrero was even wider and more dashing than she had anticipated. The holster was complete with a gleaming sharp-shooter. There was even a sparkling sheriff's badge included in the outfit.

For the girls there was an exciting assortment varying from books featuring stories of ponies and their care, to boxes of handkerchiefs printed with riding motifs and scarves stamped with pony designs. For the boys there were tooled leather belts, cowboy shirts, pistols and rifles. Helen had even baked a Christmas cake and sent it along with the other articles. Rich and dark, it was complete with snowy icing and decorated with sprigs of artificial holly. Suddenly Liz glanced up. 'Heavens, we've forgotten something, party hats!'

'Not to worry,' Evelyn said in her calm tones. 'I've got swags of crêpe paper put away. I'll run them up on the sewing machine in no time!'

But she did much more than that. Soon the big refrigerator was packed with jellies, attractive desserts and fruit drinks, while the tins in the dresser were filled with small iced cakes and miniature meat pies. Stan picked the first strawberries from his garden to serve with Evelyn's home-made ice cream.

That evening Liz decorated the tree and soon it glittered with tinsel balls and coloured streamers. Malcolm brought long branches of greenery and arranged them around the walls. He blew up balloons and anchored the clusters of floating spheres high on the rafters. Afterwards they all helped to parcel up the gifts and arrange them around the base of the small pine.

The next morning everything was in readiness. Liz planned to give only a short riding lesson today, just down the slope and over the back paddock. Then instead of being loaded back into ambulances on their return, the children would be taken in their wheelchairs to the barn.

Following the ambulances came Lewis's car. Liz could see Julie waving from the window. Smilingly Liz waved back, then her gaze slid to Lewis and unconsciously she sighed. He looked so happy, so hopeful, and still she couldn't bring herself to make a decision.

At that moment a party of medical experts approached her and she recognised among the group the lined kindly face of a specialist well known in his own country and overseas for his achievements in the treatment of children's diseases. Introductions were made, then the great man took Liz's brown hand in a friendly clasp. 'Could I have a word with you later, Miss Kennedy, when you're free?'

'Of course,' she promised, and moved towards the wheelchairs being assembled at the side of the railing where the ponies that Malcolm had already saddled stood waiting.

Immediately she was conscious of a babel of happy voices, and before long she was setting off across the paddock with the others, leading a small shaggy pony while Danny held the reins. There had been times during the past few weeks when she had despaired of his ever breaking through the barrier of fear that had grown with him through the years, yet today for the first time he was riding without the aid of helpers on either side. He really was making astonishing progress.

'Looking forward to the party, Danny?' She smiled up over her shoulder towards the thin figure in the saddle.

He nodded. 'I've been marking the days off on my

173

calendar, and do you know what, Miss Kennedy?' The hesitant weak tones had taken on a new note of confidence. 'I've got a surprise for you!'

Liz led the pony towards a group of riders ahead, some of whom were urging their mounts into a trot. 'Good for you! What is it, Danny? A Christmas gift?'

'Sort of.' The sweetness of his smile never failed to give Liz a pang. 'I think you'll like it.'

'I'm sure I will.' She was reflecting that a month ago he would never have chatted away in this fashion. He would have been far too tense and nervous to think of anything else.

As always on lesson days, the time flew by on wings. Liz had forgotten the important visitor who wished to interview her until as the second section of children were returned to their wheelchairs and Malcolm began to lead the ponies away, the distinguished man approached her.

'Congratulations, Miss Kennedy! I've been watching the children riding their ponies and to my mind,' the gentle lined face broke into a smile, 'your centre presents a perfect example of what can be achieved with this particular form of outdoor exercise. Before coming here today I spent some time in going over the medical records of these children and it's noticeable that in every case there's been a distinct improvement, physically from the exercise and psychologically from the feeling of achievement that riding gives them. In my book,' to Liz the warmly appreciative glance was akin to being handed a bouquet of fragrant roses, 'you deserve a vote of thanks from us all for what you've done in helping these handicapped children.'

'I'm glad if what I've done helps a little.' She felt a trifle overawed at the compliments of this brilliant man whose work in the field of the treatment of cerebral palsy had brought him fame all over the world.

'A little! Believe me, Miss Kennedy, your riding exercise for cases like these is more in the nature of a breakthrough! You know what we're up against in the treatment of spastic deplegia? The typical spastic scissor gait, the difficulty in getting the legs apart that

174

often violently reacts to any effort to make the muscles respond? The boy Danny is an example ... nervous strain, tense muscles. So far as mobility goes, his improvement from now on is practically a certainty—thanks to your help. You must feel very gratified, Miss Kennedy, at the success of all this!' He waved a hand towards the scene of happy activity where children and animals mingled in an atmosphere of happiness and relaxation.

'Thank you, but it's really just a beginning. You see——' She hesitated. It seemed presumptuous of her to rave on about her wider vision to this eminent visitor.

'Yes, Miss Kennedy?' The lined intelligent face was bent attentively towards her.

'I thought, in the future, if everything goes along well maybe the centre could be improved a lot. One thing I'd like to do would be to have a covered riding area made where the lessons could be taken even in bad weather.'

'An excellent suggestion.'

Encouraged by his interest, she hurried on, 'This is just a long-term project, but I've always hoped that some day when the centre is firmly established, wouldn't it be fabulous if it could be extended to include lots of other types of the disabled? Deaf, blind, all sorts—a national centre for the disabled. Of course,' she finished breathlessly, 'it's all just an idea.'

'Why not?' The great man appeared to share her enthusiasm. 'It's been done before in England, so why not here? You've made great progress already, Miss Kennedy. I want to thank you. Don't ever forget that we in the medical profession are with you all the way!'

The glow of gratification lasted all the while a group of medical experts joined their distinguished colleague in congratulating Liz on her work with the handicapped, and for a short while afterwards. But as the medical team strolled away the momentary excitement went too. It seemed that even the satisfaction of making a dream come true wasn't enough. It failed to ease the pain in her heart or to fill the sense of incompleteness that had been with her ever since she had learned the truth concerning Peter ... and Beryl. She had come a long way towards achievement of a life's ambition, but on another level—If only Peter could have been here with her today. In spite of everything, you would think he would come to see her at Christmas time, if only to wish her well. With a sigh she turned away and moved towards the cottage.

To give a more festive air to the occasion and to make the small guests feel more 'Christmassy' she changed into a long frock. The soft sea-island cotton with its high bodice and full long sleeves fell softly around her ankles, lending her an air of deceptive fragility.

When she reached the barn the children were already settled on the long forms beside the table and Malcolm, seated at the old piano, was banging out *Silent Night* on the yellowed keys. Excited shouts filled the air. 'Look, there's a Christmas tree!' 'I know—I can see my name on a parcel!' 'So can I!' 'Where's mine?' The children were unfolding crêpe paper hats, pulling them over their heads with comical effects as Liz pushed her way through the throng of helpers, a huge plate of potato chips in her hand.

'Wait!' The quietly authoritative tones of a woman therapist cut across the rising buzz of voices, gaining instant attention. 'No one's to start yet. There's someone who isn't here. Can you guess who it is?'

'It's Danny! Where's Danny?' Childish voices rose in chorus.

'Here I am, Miss Kennedy!' The high tremulous tones came from the doorway and Liz felt a lump in her throat. Danny, *on crutches*! He was moving over the floor towards her, slowly, carefully, but moving! Could this be the boy whose only way of moving had been to slither around the floor like a fish, and who for so long had resisted all efforts to help him achieve some degree of mobility? Liz didn't know whether to laugh or cry, then found she was doing both at once. In the silence as Danny tap-tapped his way slowly and painstakingly towards the table, Liz hoped and prayed that he would come to no mishap. At last he reached the long form and eager hands took the crutches from him, helped him to his seat. Liz let out her breath on a sigh of relief.

'That's marvellous, Danny!' She flew to him, hugged him tight. 'That was the best surprise I ever had! You did it, Danny! You really learned to use crutches!'

Suddenly overcome by so much attention, he hung his head, but Liz had caught the expression of pleasure and pride in the pale eyes. 'Oh, Danny, I'm so *proud* of you!'

At that moment Malcolm broke into the rhythm of Christmas carols and the children, appetites sharpened after their ride, needed no encouragement to eat with enjoyment and gusto. At last, when most of the plates on the table were emptied, Liz heard the pop of a champagne cork and looking up, realised that Lewis was pouring the sparkling liquid into chipped cups, for they had run out of glasses. He handed them around until medical officers, therapists, drivers and helpers each held a cup. 'To Liz and her riding school! May she have many more successes!'

'To Liz!'

Across the room her glance met his look of pride, and something warmer, for his eyes signalled a secret message. Her glance slid away. At this moment only one name filled her thoughts. If only Peter were here to share it all with her! Time enough when the children had gone to force her reluctant thoughts back to Lewis, and the answer to his proposal that she *must* give him today. The rousing strains of *For She's a Jolly Good Fellow* cut across her thoughts and she realised that all eyes were turned in her direction. Laughingly she disclaimed the applause. 'Not just me, you know! Everyone else was in it too. Don't forget all the helpers, the therapists, the medical people—and of course the ambulance drivers. You've all been wonderful,' smilingly her gaze moved towards Malcolm, 'and that goes for the pianist too!'

Soon she was helping to push wheelchairs towards

the Christmas tree, watching as with shrieks of delight, the children opened up their gifts.

Suddenly, above the din, rose a child's scream. 'Look, everybody! It's Father Christmas!'

Jingle Bells! Jingle Bells! thundered Malcolm from his seat at the piano. Liz, gazing in astonishment, recognised Wayne and Tim. With paper party hats pulled over sun-tanned faces and lustily blowing tin whistles, they were running across the room pulling, behind them a sled wherein sat a smiling, red-cloaked Santa Claus. The sled paused beside Liz and she found herself meeting hazel eyes with a familiar glint.

'It's *you!*' she whispered.

'It's me all right and it's damned hot behind these whiskers,' came a sibilant whisper from the bearded face. 'Don't blame me for all this——' He threw a glance towards the bulging sack behind him. 'We got wind on the grapevine of your show today and Beryl wanted to help, so—I'll tell you this much,' came the low mutter from lips almost hidden by the flowing white beard, 'I wouldn't have done it for any other girl!' He meant Beryl, of course. His tone rose to a jovial shout. 'Right, kids!' Stepping from the sled, Peter moved among the cluster of wheelchairs, handing each child a gift taken from the giant sack. 'Boy, girl ... boy, girl ...' Riotous cheers and calls all but drowned his voice. But what expensive gifts, Liz thought, taking in the china tea-sets, huge lifelike dolls and battery-driven toys that the children were taking from professionally-wrapped parcels. They must have cost the earth. All at once the carefully-selected gifts that had been heaped beneath the sturdy little pine seemed awfully cheap and ordinary.

'Look!' As all eyes turned towards the open doorway Liz glanced towards the resplendent fairylike figure standing poised in the opening. Even without the long golden curls of a blonde wig she would have recognised those palest of blue eyes. 'Meet the Puppet Girl,' the red-cloaked figure was saying. 'She's come along here today to entertain you, show you what her animal puppets can do!'

Liz was forced to admit that the other girl manipulated the puppets with amazing dexterity and the childishly high tones added to the illusion. She remembered hearing that when Beryl had lived in the district previously she had taken the lead in amateur theatricals that had been held in the nearest township. But why must she come and take the lead *here*? Liz thought uncharitably, for in some indefinable way the other girl appeared to have taken over, usurping Liz's place at the celebration, spoiling the children's pleasure in their simple gifts.

At length, amidst thunderous applause, Beryl completed the show and returned the glove puppets to their box. 'And now—Surprise! Surprise!' From a carton she lifted a great three-tiered Christmas cake, intricately iced, and set it on the table.

As Liz caught the 'Ohs' and 'Ahs' of delight, she told herself she should be glad her small guests were so pleased. She would be too, if only the great iced confection hadn't the effect of making Helen's home-made cake look so small, almost pathetic. Oh, damn, what was the matter with her that she was allowing Beryl's well-meant efforts to get under her skin? In her heart she knew that had the donor been anyone else but Beryl she wouldn't feel this bitter resentment. There was no time for personal feelings, however, for voices were crying impatiently: 'When are you going to cut the cake, the BIG cake?'

'Shall I?' Nothing could be more sweetly deferring than Beryl's honeyed tones as she stood at the table, knife poised.

'Go ahead.' Liz was feeling cross and mean and hating herself for it.

'Wait! Wait!' shrilled Julie's high, piercing tones. 'Don't forget the mistletoe!'

'Where? Where?' The children peered upwards.

'There! Up high, on the middle rafter. I threw it up there among the tree branches, and that means you have to kiss someone underneath it, Miss Kennedy!'

'Hear, hear!' called the ambulance drivers.

Liz was aware of Lewis, hurrying across the room

179

towards her, but before he could reach her side his way was blocked by a tall figure. Peter was standing facing her. He had shed his crimson robes and the way he was looking at her . . .

'A kiss under the mistletoe, Miss Kennedy!' The chorus of childish voices blurred and she was aware of nothing but his dark and brilliant gaze.

'You heard?' Before she could make her escape he had caught her close, then his arms tightened around her and she felt his lips on hers. Pulses leaping, she was seized by a trembling excitement and for all she knew to the contrary Malcolm's honky-tonk tune could have been the singing of a thousand violins. A moment, a minute—she had no idea of how long she stayed in his embrace before he gently released her. She was aware only of ecstasy and longing and anguish.

A peal of childish laughter splintered the moment to fragments. 'It wasn't *really* mistletoe!' Julie's high tones shrilled above the babel of voices. 'It was just old pohutukawa from the tree outside tied with one of my old red hair ribbons, but Daddy said it would do!'

In the ensuing burst of good-natured merriment she was aware of Peter's intent glance. 'Too late.' She never could guess what he was thinking. Her cheeks were burning while he appeared as cool and collected as ever. Why not? Just a Christmas kiss. If only he hadn't noticed her wild response to his nearness, would put down her heightened colour to the heat of the crowded room.

Breathlessly she turned away, to surprise an angry gleam in Beryl's pale eyes. The momentary expression was gone in a flash and now the lovely face was smiling. 'My goodness! I can see I'll have to keep an eye on you, Peter, from now on!'

Vaguely Liz was aware that Malcolm's touch had faltered on the piano keys, and like everyone else in the room, he was watching her.

'Don't worry,' said Liz, and bit back the words that trembled on her lips. 'You've nothing to fear from me.' All at once a wave of angry frustration swept her and the hot tears stung her eyelids. Why should Beryl have everything? Why did Peter mock her with his love-making that to him meant nothing but a moment's amusement, a fun-thing?

'Too bad I missed out!' In her blind misery she was scarcely aware of Lewis or of the deep disappointment in his grey eyes. It seemed that he was fated to be always at hand when she needed him, ready to pick up the pieces!

Automatically she began to catch the balloons that Malcolm had released from the ceiling beams and which were now drifting down to the floor. She handed them to the children to take back to town with them, but all the time she was aware of Peter. He was standing at Beryl's side, her golden curls brushing his shoulder, and they were laughing together at some shared secret joke. Well, let them laugh! She didn't care! A bitter recklessness surged through her. She didn't care about anything! Let Beryl smile her cruel smile, Peter play his meaningless game of love! She would make a life of her own in spite of them! They'd be a family, she and Lewis, she thought wildly. Funny to think of being a family all at once. She was trying desperately to convince herself, arguing away the flicker of doubt that she didn't want to acknowledge, not with Peter's kiss still burning on her lips.

'Looks like it's all over.' Lewis's tone was low and intimate. Together they watched as children, each clutching a paper hat, a balloon and various gifts, were wheeled away. He caught her fingers in swift and urgent pressure. 'Liz, you haven't forgotten——'

'Later.' At that moment to her relief she found herself surrounded by groups of children and adults, all calling farewells and extending thanks for the end-of-term celebration.

Tim and Wayne, the two station-hands from Arundel, thrust out work-grained hands. 'Great to see you again, Liz!' Both sun-tanned faces were grinning engagingly.

'Almost worth yanking the boss around the place in that flipping sled,' Wayne put in.

'We'll see you in the New Year!'

They moved aside and she found herself looking directly into Beryl's smiling features. Liz heard herself murmuring the conventional phrases, 'Thanks for your help. The children enjoyed the puppet show.' She scarcely listened to the other girl's words. What was she saying? Something concerning Darryl. 'Thought he might have arrived here by now. He said something about coming over for a ride after the party. Something must have come up and made him change his mind.'

If only she'd go, Liz thought. She felt she never wanted to see Beryl again.

At length everyone appeared to have departed, the private cars forming a long line behind the two ambulances that were moving up the winding road. Now only one vehicle remained on the grass—Peter's long grey car. In spite of herself her heart plunged as he came towards her.

'That was a great show you put on today, and did those kids enjoy it!'

'Thanks for coming,' she whispered, 'and for being such a good Father Christmas.'

'It was darned hot, that outfit, but I guess it was worth it to see the look on those kids' faces when we made the big entrance scene.'

(Not as pleased as I was to see you, Peter, but you'll never know about that.) Aloud she heard herself say in a cool, polite, *uncaring* tone, 'Was it . . . your idea?'

He nodded, his eyes never leaving her face. 'I found the fancy dress outfit and the white whiskers in one of the rooms at the house, the boys knocked the sled together, shoved a coat of red paint on it and we were in business—when can I see you again, Liz?'

She hesitated. How easy it would be to fall into the old trap! 'I don't know,' she murmured vaguely. 'Some time.'

'What's wrong with tonight?'

'No, sorry . . . Lewis is coming over.'

The gaiety died out of his face in an instant, leaving the hazel eyes as cold as river pebbles. The look he slanted her was cutting. 'I get it. Well, so long, Liz. Be seeing you.'

But he wouldn't, she thought. It was the last time he would ever ask her out. From now on there would always be Lewis ... and Beryl.

' 'Bye.' She turned away before he could glimpse the bleakness that must surely show in her face for all her efforts to hide her anguish.

He didn't glance back, why should he? She watched him seat himself in the car, the pain in her heart like a knife. At first the barking of the dogs failed to register in her mind then she realised that the wild clamour must mean that something was wrong. The next moment she caught the sound of galloping hoofs on the road approaching the cottage and even as she glanced towards the entrance a riderless horse swerved in at the opening, swept past the car in the driveway and came to an abrupt halt at her side.

'Red!' He was flecked with foam and wet with sea-water. A broken bridle trailed in the dust. She glanced up to meet Peter's enquiring look. His voice was sharp. 'Did you know someone had him out today?'

'No, but——'

'Are you thinking what I'm thinking? Young Darryl——'

'Peter! You don't think he could——' Her eyes widened as the frightening supposition flashed into her mind.

'Don't worry. He's probably bailed out on the way home! Come on, jump into the car!' she sensed the urgency in his tone. 'We'll go take a look and see if we can pick him up.'

She paused only to call over her shoulder to Stan, who had strolled into sight at that moment and was staring in surprise at the horse's wet coat. 'Someone had him out. We think it may have been Darryl. Will you give Beryl a ring? Tell her we'll bring him back as soon as we find him.' Even as she spoke the vehicle was leaping ahead and in a moment had swung into the main highway. A swift glance along the ferny verges of the road showed no sign of anyone lying there, nor was there any sign of life along the lonely, bush-fringed road ahead.

'We'll take a look down at the beach!' Peter told her. They were travelling at high speed and Liz knew that the same terrifying possibility filled both their minds. If the boy had been tossed into the wild surf below . . .

'At least he can swim,' she voiced her thoughts. 'He always wanted to take Red down into the tide and Beryl told me today that she was expecting him to come over this afternoon for a ride. He must have taken a chance on helping himself to Red when we were all busy down in the barn with the party——'

'He's taken a bigger chance than that if he's out in the surf today.' Peter's tone was grim. 'I put a broadcast over the air this morning to swimmers, warning them of danger. A heck of a lot of deep holes appeared during the night, and now with this strong rip . . . he couldn't have chosen a worse time for his dip!'

They lurched into a winding overgrown track leading down the cliff to the beach below. Tree branches scraped the car roof as they swept on beneath overhanging tea-tree and stones flew up from the undercarriage. At last they jolted down on to black sand and leaping from the car, Peter scanned the tossing sea.

'There he is!'

Peering over his shoulder, Liz could at first see only a turbulent sea, then in a trough in the waves she glimpsed a fair head. She caught her breath. 'He's an awfully long way out.'

'Come on!' They were in the car and speeding over the sand in the direction of the clubhouse. Even before they reached the small building perched on the rocks they caught the chop-chop of a helicopter overhead.

As Peter ran towards the building a bronzed young figure appeared on the look-out platform. 'It's all right! We've phoned for a chopper. Here he comes now.'

'Right! I'll go up with him!' Already Peter was peeling off outer garments and as the machine swooped low on the sand he swung himself aboard.

'How long is it since you noticed Darryl out there?' Liz spoke to the young life-saver without taking her eyes from the machine that was moving so swiftly towards the bobbing head out among the waves.

'Darryl? Is that who it is? I saw a hand raised in the signal for help about ten minutes ago.' The gaze of the man too was fixed on the hovering machine. 'But he wasn't so far out at sea then. I could see right away that it was going to be a tough rescue, the rip would carry him out in no time, so I rang right away for the 'copter.'

'He took one of my horses and went into the surf.'

'Is that what he was up to? I didn't see the horse. It must have taken off for home by then, but I can make a good guess at what happened. The horse must have stumbled into one of the deep holes in the sand and tossed him off. After that, with the tide against him and this dangerous rip, he'd be lucky if he ever made the shore again! Now it's up to Peter and he'll soon have him aboard the 'copter. There he goes! He's put in a lot of practice this season jumping into the sea from one of those!'

Liz didn't answer. She was holding her breath as a figure dropped down, down into the tossing waves beneath. It seemed to her an age before rescuer and rescued, clinging to a lifeline beneath the machine, were dragged from the sea.

Then the 'copter was heading towards the beach and only then did she realise that others too had come to wait beside her on the sand. Beryl, still wearing her wig of golden curls, was clinging to Sandy's arm and near at hand stood Evelyn and Stan. It was a silent group. All were eyeing the machine now dropping down to the beach. As it touched the sand Sandy hurried forward and soon he was carrying Darryl towards the waiting car.

'How is he, Peter?' Liz had never seen Beryl like this, ashen-faced, white-lipped. 'Will he——'

'He'll be okay. He's under the weather a bit at the moment from shock and exposure, but a day or two's rest will soon fix that.'

'You're all right, Darryl!' She burst into tears and ran to fling her arms around the boy.

'Aw, Mum, I'm okay,' he mumbled. 'If old Red hadn't gone into a hole——'

'Take him home,' Peter said. 'A hot drink is what he needs right now. Some dry clothes. Keep him warm, make him rest.'

'Oh, I will! I will!' Beryl turned to Sandy and Liz caught the tremulous tones. 'Will you drive, please, Sandy? I don't feel up to it today.' Release from tension appeared to have rendered the other girl vulnerable to emotion, for she was laughing and crying as she clung to Sandy's arm. 'Darling, darling, you were right all the time!' Darling ... Liz could scarcely believe her ears. 'I knew you were, but I just wouldn't let myself come right out and admit it. He *does* need a firm hand! He needs you, Sandy, *and so do I*!' The tears ran unchecked down her cheeks. 'You know what it is I'm trying to say, don't you?'

'I know, honey.' His deep tones conveyed an intimacy that Liz failed to understand.

He had tucked a rug around the boy lying on the back seat of the car and now he climbed in behind the steering wheel. But still Beryl's high tones ran on. She seemed determined to make everything clear between them, regardless of who overheard her confidences. 'It's going to be all different from now on,' the words spilled from her trembling lips as she seated herself beside Sandy. 'No more pretending I'm crazy about Peter and he about me just to try to make you feel jealous! He knows as well as I do that all that was finished years ago! From now on it's you, Sandy. You're the boss!'

'Let's go home, honey.' Sandy laid a hand on her fingers for a moment, then started the engine. As the car moved up the cliff path it was followed by Evelyn and Stan in their battered Holden. When the 'copter had taken off again, Peter said to Liz, 'Wait for me, will you, while I change in the clubhouse?' He was back in a few minutes, wearing a dry shirt and shorts, his thick dark hair curling wetly against the back of

186

his neck. There wasn't anyone to compare with him, Liz was thinking, not in all the world! Not for her anyway! Yet she still couldn't really believe ...

'I'll see you home,' he was saying.

'But aren't you going up to the house ... with them?'

He tossed back damp hair. 'Good grief, no! They don't want me around, especially just now! Didn't you hear what Beryl was telling Sandy?'

A wild hope sang in her heart and she could scarcely catch his words for the excitement that was surging through her.

'It mightn't be a bad thing at that, young Darryl getting himself half drowned. Might teach him a lesson that he can't go throwing his weight around all the time and get away with it! It just needed something like this to fix things for those two! Beryl and Sandy will be great for each other, but I guess it took a real shock to make her see reason, get her to finally make up her mind——'

'About what?'

'Teaming up with Sandy, of course. What else?' It was his turn to look mystified. 'I got the idea that you'd caught on to that ages ago.'

'No——'

'Every time Sandy tried to use a bit of discipline with Darryl, Beryl flew into a state and all the marriage plans were off. I should know! Only the other day I got an urgent message to rush over to her place. Big decision. Would I act as best man at the wedding? Next week they were arguing over Darryl again and everything was back to square one. He just couldn't get it through to Beryl that she was making the mistake of her life in giving in to the boy on every count. The kid needs a father, and a strong one at that. That's what she was getting at just now when she told Sandy that he'd been on the right track all along. So it's happy endings for them, thanks to a near accident.'

Liz continued to stare up at him, amazement and an almost unbelievable happiness surging through her. Vaguely she was aware that everyone, even the bronzed young life-saver, had gone. The long black stretch of sand was left to the wheeling gulls, and there was only Peter, regarding her with a sudden bleak expression in his hazel eyes. 'You ... and Lewis——'

'But I thought,' being Liz she had to blurt out the thoughts that were clamouring in her mind, 'that you and Beryl ... that it was *you*——'

He gripped her arm in so fierce a grip that she could feel the pain, or would have had she not been so filled with a soaring excitement to be unaware of anything else.

'Tell me, Liz,' his voice was ragged with emotion, so low she was forced to strain to catch the words, 'would it have made any difference, if you'd known? They tell me that you and Lewis are getting engaged any day——'

'Not now! Not ever!'

'*What!*' He was the Peter she had known at first, alive, vibrant, *hers*! 'I love you so much——' She didn't hear any more because her senses were drowned in his kiss.

Lost in the intoxication of the moment, neither was aware of the car that had drawn to a stop on the path directly above them. Nor did they notice a grim-faced man who stood silently observing them from the cliff. Only for a moment, then sunlight caught the flash of jewels as the ring he had held in his hands went hurtling through the shimmering air to vanish in a trough in the waves among the blue depths below. Turning on his heel, Lewis got back into his car and drove away.

But Liz heard only Peter's deep tones. 'You couldn't marry anyone else, Liz. You belonged to me from the first moment we met, and you know it!'

She murmured from the ineffable comfort of his arms. 'A drowned rat——'

'An adorable drowned rat! But I'm not going to take any chances of letting you go out of my life again, ever. Marry me, Liz. Stay here with me!'

She stirred in his embrace, smiling up into his eyes.

'You have to take the kids too, and the horses, and probably Evelyn and Stan as well——'

'What of it? The kids are your department, sweet,' lightly he caressed her dark hair, 'with a little help from me, of course.' He kissed her again. 'You can come over the hills from Arundel any old time to see how things are running. Stan and Evelyn can keep an eye on the place when you're not there. It'll work out, you'll see!'

She sighed contentedly. 'Wonderful! I couldn't give up the riding centre, not now. But to have someone to share it with, someone who understands. You know, Mr. X won't ever know that he's not the most important man in my life any more——'

'Don't bet on it!'

As she caught his teasing grin a number of puzzling matters suddenly sorted themselves out and clicked neatly into place. Drawing herself free, she stared up at him accusingly. 'It was *you*, all the time——'

'Do you mind?' His low exultant laugh as once again he sought her lips put everything else from her mind. A little later she gazed into his glinting eyes. 'I might have known! So that was why the cheques always came through a solicitor, and I never got a personal letter back in reply to my "thank-you" notes. I didn't ever think,' she marvelled, 'that you were all that interested.'

'I was always interested.' His tone was deep and soft and infinitely caressing. 'It was all part of the girl I love.'

Love. Liz's heart was a wild tumult of emotion. It was coming home after a long, long time. It was setting out on the biggest adventure of all, but not alone, not ever alone again. Always they'd be together, she and Peter!

FREE! Harlequin Romance Catalogue

Here is a wonderful opportunity to read many of the Harlequin Romances you may have missed.

The HARLEQUIN ROMANCE CATALOGUE lists hundreds of titles which possibly are no longer available at your local bookseller. To receive your copy, just fill out the coupon below, mail it to us, and we'll rush your catalogue to you!

Following this page you'll find a sampling of a few of the Harlequin Romances listed in the catalogue. Should you wish to order any of these immediately, kindly check the titles desired and mail with coupon.

To: **HARLEQUIN READER SERVICE, Dept. N 305**
    M.P.O. Box 707, Niagara Falls, N.Y. 14302
    Canadian address: Stratford, Ont., Canada

☐ Please send me the free Harlequin Romance Catalogue.

☐ Please send me the titles checked.

I enclose $_____ (No C.O.D.'s), All books are 60c each. To help defray postage and handling cost, please add 25c.

Name _____

Address _____

City/Town _____

State/Prov. _____ Zip_____

Have You Missed Any of These
Harlequin Romances?

All books are 60c. Please use the handy order coupon.

AA

Have You Missed Any of These Harlequin Romances?

- [ ] 412 NURSE TRENTON
  Caroline Trench
- [ ] 416 DOCTOR LUCY
  Barbara Allen
- [ ] 423 NURSE GREVE
  Jane Arbor
- [ ] 434 DEAR DOCTOR EVERETT
  Jean S. Macleod
- [ ] 799 LOVE IS FOR EVER
  Barbara Rowan
- [ ] 908 ELIZABETH BROWNE,
  CHILDREN'S NURSE
  Rosalind Brett
- [ ] 922 THE TAMING OF NURSE
  CONWAY
  Nora Sanderson
- [ ] 1031 FLOWERING DESERT
  Elizabeth Hoy
- [ ] 1182 GOLDEN APPLE ISLAND
  Jane Arbor
- [ ] 1183 NEVER CALL IT LOVING
  Marjorie Lewty
- [ ] 1184 THE HOUSE OF OLIVER
  Jean S. Macleod
- [ ] 1211 BRIDE OF KYLSAIG
  Iris Danbury
- [ ] 1226 HONEYMOON HOLIDAY
  Elizabeth Hoy
- [ ] 1242 NEW DOCTOR AT NORTHMOOR
  Anne Durham
- [ ] 1307 A CHANCE TO WIN
  Margaret Rome
- [ ] 1308 A MIST IN GLEN TORRAN
  Amanda Doyle
- [ ] 1310 TAWNY ARE THE LEAVES
  Wynne May
- [ ] 1311 THE MARRIAGE WHEEL
  Susan Barrie
- [ ] 1312 PEPPERCORN HARVEST
  Ivy Ferrari
- [ ] 1314 SUMMER ISLAND
  Jean S. Macleod
- [ ] 1316 CAN THIS BE LOVE
  Margaret Malcolm
- [ ] 1317 BELOVED SPARROW
  Henrietta Reid
- [ ] 1320 SPANISH LACE
  Joyce Dingwell
- [ ] 1325 NO SOONER LOVED
  Pauline Garner

- [ ] 1327 MORE THAN GOLD
  Hilda Pressley
- [ ] 1328 A WIND SIGHING
  Catherine Airlie
- [ ] 1330 A HOME FOR JOY
  Mary Burchell
- [ ] 1331 HOTEL BELVEDERE
  Iris Danbury
- [ ] 1332 DON'T WALK ALONE
  Jane Donnelly
- [ ] 1333 KEEPER OF THE HEART
  Gwen Westwood
- [ ] 1334 THE DAMASK ROSE
  Isobel Chace
- [ ] 1336 THE CYPRESS GARDEN
  Jane Arbor
- [ ] 1338 SEA OF ZANJ   Roumelia Lane
- [ ] 1339 SLAVE OF THE WIND
  Jean S. Macleod
- [ ] 1341 FIRE IS FOR SHARING
  Doris E. Smith
- [ ] 1342 THE FEEL OF SILK
  Joyce Dingwell
- [ ] 1344 THE DANGEROUS DELIGHT
  Violet Winspear
- [ ] 1352 THE MOUNTAIN OF STARS
  Catherine Airlie
- [ ] 1357 RIPPLES IN THE LAKE
  Mary Coates
- [ ] 1393 HEALER OF HEARTS
  Katrina Britt
- [ ] 1400 THE DISTANT TRAP
  Gloria Bevan
- [ ] 1411 TURN THE PAGE
  Nan Asquith
- [ ] 1413 THE FAMILY FACE
  Bethea Creese
- [ ] 1430 HUNTER'S MOON
  Henrietta Reid
- [ ] 1431 THE OTHER LINDING GIRL
  Mary Burchell
- [ ] 1433 THE PURSUIT OF DR. LLOYD
  Marjorie Norrell
- [ ] 1448 THE YEAR AT YATTABILLA
  Amanda Doyle
- [ ] 1450 HEIR TO GLEN GHYLL
  Lucy Gillen
- [ ] 1453 THE BENEVOLENT DESPOT
  Elizabeth Ashton
- [ ] 1458 THE ENCHANTED ISLAND
  Eleanor Farnes

All books are 60c. Please use the handy order coupon.

BB